'What is it? What's the matter?'

But he knew what it was without her reply. She was feeling what he'd felt on first seeing her earlier today—a sense of recognition so powerful it had resonated throughout his body.

And he knew the next move was inevitable.

With a stifled moan, he bent his head and kissed her, finding her lips, parted by surprise, easy to access. His tongue explored the soft warm cave of her mouth, tasting honey, flowers, sweet heady wine, and most of all—strangest of all—familiarity.

'Ellie?' he murmured, lifting his lips from hers so he could look at her again—marvelling at what was happening.

She stared up at him, her eyes mirroring the amazement he was feeling, then the smallest hint of a smile danced across her lips and his mouth was forced to capture them again, in case, in smiling, their taste might have altered.

Writers can write anywhere. **Meredith Webber** proved that when she moved to a caravan in a small country town in central Queensland. The idea was to see if she and her husband would enjoy living in a place they'd previously only visited. They did— enough to buy a house and settle into a totally different lifestyle. Why central Queensland? The area is rich in minerals and gemstones, but it's the gold that interests the Webbers. Spare time finds them out fossicking, searching the abandoned diggings for scraps the old-timers left behind. It's great exercise, a terrific challenge, and provides plenty of solitude and 'thinking time' for plots and characters.

Recent titles by the same author:

THE DOCTOR'S CHRISTMAS FAMILY
DOCTOR AND PROTECTOR
DOCTORS IN PARADISE

THE GREEK DOCTOR'S RESCUE

BY
MEREDITH WEBBER

MILLS & BOON®

MILLS & BOON and
MILLS & BOON with the Rose Device
are registered trademarks of the publisher.

First published in Great Britain 2005
Large Print edition 2005
Harlequin Mills & Boon Limited,
Eton House, 18-24 Paradise Road,
Richmond, Surrey TW9 1SR

© Meredith Webber 2005

ISBN 0 263 18477 3

Set in Times Roman 16 on 17 pt.
17-0905-53555

Printed and bound in Great Britain
by Antony Rowe Ltd, Chippenham, Wiltshire

CHAPTER ONE

ERIREKA appeared as a tiny speck of darkest emerald green set in a jewel-bright sea. Coral reefs beneath the ocean's surface painted swirls of jade and cobalt in the blue-green water, while the shallows, washing over brilliant white coral sand, were pale, translucent aqua.

The speck grew larger as the plane descended, appearing as a steep and rugged peak, the lower slopes clad with jungle, giving the impression a thick green blanket had been wrapped around the barren rock.

To warm it?

Nikos Conias, muscles and sinews tense with the frustration from the delays he'd experienced, and the seemingly interminable journey to the island, shook his head at the fanciful notion. The equatorial air of Erireka would do all the warming necessary. This was a place that knew no winter, and, until comparatively recent times, had known no other hardships. Off the tourist route, the Erirekans had been able to ignore the outside world for far longer than the rest of their neighbours in the South Pacific.

Was that what he was doing here? Ignoring the outside world? The real world? Ellie Reardon had once accused him of using his work in war zones and famine-stricken areas as an escape, though she'd denied the same applied to herself...

The thought of seeing Ellie again lightened his dark mood—though only momentarily as he remembered he always looked forward to meeting up with her, then within minutes of the reunion they'd be arguing and he'd recall just what a stubborn, self-willed, obdurate and infuriating woman she was.

Ellie...

A huff of self-mocking laughter escaped his lips, as he remembered, also, how close he'd come to making a fool of himself over her.

But that was in the past, and this time she was right. His trip to Erireka was definitely an escape—two months of freedom from decisions and family responsibilities.

The memories of the past month—the month since his father's death—pressed heavily on his shoulders, but he refused to think about the situation he'd left behind, turning his mind deliberately to what he knew of the island nation.

Although missionaries had found their way to the shores, building a church and starting a school, for the most part the island and its people had remained untouched. With nothing of value for early traders and with an encircling reef that had kept whaling and black-birding ships at bay, Erireka had lived on as an anachronism in the modern world until well into the twentieth century, when some desperate gambler had landed on its shores and by sheer chance had discovered deposits of platinum so rich the largest conglomerates in the world had fought for the rights to mine it.

The winning company had blasted an opening in the protective reef, dredged out a harbour, built a wharf and started mining.

They'd sent ore to Canada on bulk carriers that sailed under the Blue Funnel flag—the Blue Funnel flag designed by his father and his father's best friend, Nikos Pippos, back when the pair had first gone into commercial shipping. The part of Nik's brain that refused to forget business reminded him of this minor complication, and a little of his pent-up anger over the delays, and frustration over the travel arrangements, released itself in a long sigh.

Get a grip! he told himself. You've got two months before you have to think about the shipping company, so put it right out of your head. Concentrate on Erireka. Think about what you know or have learnt about the place—things that might help the mission.

It took a huge mental effort, but he refocused determinedly. With the mine had come modernisation. Pre-fabricated housing had replaced the traditional village bures and the Erirekans had learnt new words—electricity, democracy, supermarket, television.

Nik held his breath as the plane skirted precariously close to the base of the mountain and zeroed in on the narrow airstrip. Electricity, supermarkets and television had all been embraced by the island people, but the democracy idea hadn't been adopted as enthusiastically. The mining company had pulled out when the fighting had escalated from occasional raids by so-called guerrillas to full-scale war between two different factions, both claiming sovereignty over the land that held the ore. Local leaders had tried to run the mine themselves, but without contacts in the outside world their venture had failed, causing more anger among the islanders.

The plane dropped suddenly, bounced twice as its wheels connected with the ground, then taxied along the runway, the encroaching jungle so close Nik wondered how long it would be before nature reclaimed the airfield. As they rolled to a halt, armed figures in military fatigues swarmed out of the small terminal building.

'I hope these are the good guys,' Nik said, and the pilot, who had completed his shut-down and walked back into the cabin, grinned at him.

'Doesn't make much difference!' he said. 'Depends who's on top. This month's good guys, might be the bad guys next month. It's one of those stupid situations where everyone loses.'

He paused then added, 'Especially the kids. If it weren't for the kids, I wouldn't come near the place, but since the island went modern, and the men took to fighting instead of fishing and tending their plots and livestock, the kids'd starve to death without the food I bring in.'

He unlatched the cabin door and pushed it outwards, releasing the steps at the same time.

'Sounds like we might be really needed here.' Jack Lee, an elderly handyman who'd attached himself to Nik five years earlier, had straightened out of his seat and moved towards the door, making the comment to Nik as he passed.

Nik stood up and stretched, wondering if he'd ever get the kinks out of his back after a four-hour flight in what must be one of the most ancient aircraft still flying. Who'd ever heard of canvas seats in a plane?

'Much as I wouldn't wish ill on anyone, man, woman or child,' he grumbled, 'I'd hate to think we *weren't* needed and I'd endured that flight for nothing! Orville and Wilbur would have flown in greater comfort.'

'Orville and Wilbur didn't have to ditch the regular seating to pack in extra supplies,' the pilot, returning to the cabin with a couple of soldiers, reminded him. 'These guys will help you unload and see you safely to the camp.'

He flashed a wolfish smile as he sidled closer to Nik.

'At least, that's where they say they'll take you,' he murmured.

The taller of the two soldiers approached. A well-built man, with healthily shining skin and crinkly black hair turning into dreadlocks, he introduced himself as Arwon.

'Your other workers are already settled at the camp,' he said, soothing the vague unease the pilot's words had caused. 'They are using the cabins brought in by the mining company. The mining company stole our ore but they left some useful things. Even food.'

He laughed as if delighted by the hasty departure of the mining personnel when civil unrest had erupted across the island, before turning to Jack and asking which cases should be unloaded first.

'Those over there. And treat them all as breakable,' Jack suggested. 'There are sensitive medical instruments in them.'

Nik found his own gear—duffelbag, backpack, a case of operating equipment and his personal medical bag. He carried them down the steps, the humid tropical air bringing sweat out across his skin as he looked around, and finally felt the familiar sizzle of excitement about what might lie ahead—a feeling that had been lacking during his delayed preparations.

A soldier used his rifle to beckon him towards a battered old truck that appeared to be the only vehicle at the airfield. Nik crossed towards him. Should he dump his bags into the back of it? Leave them there while he went back to the plane to help with the unloading?

The soldiers, close to, looked more like kids playing dressing up, their 'uniforms' bits and pieces of anything vaguely military, though the flowered sarong-type garment one of the youths was wearing in place of trousers didn't quite fit with the very authentic-looking rifle he was carrying.

Deciding he had to trust someone, Nik slung his gear onto the tray of the vehicle and headed back towards the plane, passing the pilot, Jack and the first two soldiers all labouring under cases of supplies and equipment.

Forty minutes later the plane was unloaded. The pilot shook hands, wished them luck, repeated instructions given earlier for contacting him by radio, then, promising to return in a fortnight, he strode back towards his aircraft.

'That fellow's in too much of a hurry to get out of here for me to feel entirely comfortable,' Jack muttered, as the young soldier boys all piled into the cabin of the truck, leaving Nik and Jack with no alternative but to hoist themselves into the back with the gear.

'I'll find us something soft to sit on,' Nik said. 'From the look of this vehicle, the roads aren't up to much.'

He dragged his duffelbag up against the cabin so he could rest his back, shuffling around to make room for Jack.

'I wonder if the others had to travel this way, and, if so, what they made of it,' Jack said, as the engine roared and the vehicle took off with a series of bounds before settling into what seemed, given the state of the roads, to be a maniacal pace.

'Most of them have worked in post-war zones in other developing countries and know not to expect too much,' Nik reminded him, but Jack's remark made him wonder.

When he'd originally put together a medical team to visit Erireka, he'd intended being on the island before any of the volunteers arrived, but his father's death had caused an unavoidable delay so the other doctor, four nurses, a cook and two support workers who made up the team had been on the island for a fortnight.

It wasn't that he was worried about them. He'd worked with Frank Butler, the doctor, in Afghanistan, and was confident the older man would have taken the reins. Or he'd have made out he was the boss, while Ellie organised everyone to within an inch of their lives.

Nik had first met Ellie when she'd been working for Care Australia in Afghanistan and he'd been with UNESCO. Tall and slim, with an upright carriage, she'd been dressed in a traditional Muslim burka—a long shapeless faded blue garment that fell from her shoulders to her toes, though, instead of the usual Afghan head covering with its latticed window, she'd worn a headscarf wound around her head.

He'd taken her for an Afghan woman, so had been surprised to hear her clear, crisp voice berating a hapless fellow worker in unaccented English. Maybe a little accented! He'd soon picked up on some Australianisms in her speech, in particular her casual and frequent use of the Aussie adjective 'bloody', which she favoured indiscriminately so things could be either 'bloody wonderful' or 'bloody horrific'.

He'd been attracted to her, but something in the way she'd treated him—friendly and courteous, when she hadn't been arguing, but somehow aloof—had held him back from declaring this interest. Later, when he'd heard her story, he'd understood she'd built a protective blockade around her emotional self, repelling any advances.

So they'd become friends instead of lovers and though he still felt twinges of disappointment when he thought of her, he looked forward to catching up with her again. *And* to seeing the reaction of the locals when her customary quiet dignity switched to white-hot anger at perceived injustices. Yes, Ellie would have things organised!

The support workers and two of the nurses had also been part of another team he'd put together, when his idea for KidCare had first become a reality. As the only medical team on the ground in Erireka, they would, of course, be treating adults as well, but as a paediatrician his primary focus would always be the mental and physical welfare of children. Although he had volunteered the team to help out at the refugee camp, the prime aim of this mission was to set up a clinic in the town, mainly to care for mothers and children—and to train local people to carry on with the work once the team departed.

Safe childbirth procedures, good nutrition for pregnant women and children, immunisation, preventing contamination of water supplies—these things and more could be left in the hands of trained local staff who didn't need to be doctors or nurses to follow through with a programme, which would continue to be funded by KidCare.

Probably continue to be funded by KidCare…

'I wonder how the kids have been coping.' Jack must have been reading his mind!

'The same way they always cope,' Nik replied. 'Taking one day at a time. Blotting out the ugly stuff as much as they can. Remember Johnnie?'

Jack nodded, and Nik wondered if either of them would ever forget the two-year-old they'd found clinging to his dead mother's body in a burnt-out vehicle wreck outside Kabul—one small survivor among fourteen people who'd been travelling in the old army Jeep when it had run off the narrow road and plunged down a stony hillside into a ravine. From the state of the bodies, Johnnie had been keeping vigil beside his mother for at least three days—his own survival a miracle that had raised the spirits of all the volunteers working in the area.

But that was another country—a barren, dusty place with air that seemed to drag the life force out of you. Erireka burgeoned with growth, the jungle crowding the road along which they travelled, the air they breathed hot and damp.

Perfect breeding ground for infection...

The truck jolted along a narrow, shadowy road, which, like the airfield, appeared to be losing its battle with the encroaching wilderness, then suddenly they were in sunlight, driving along the top of the great open scar the mining company had left in the ground.

The road dipped around the side of the opencut mine, then turned in through what must once have been a high, wire-mesh security fence. Now the wire-mesh sagged and posts had been flattened, so it was nothing more than another ugliness in a place of great natural beauty.

They passed a row of shipping containers, with children playing around them.

Accommodation? Nik shuddered at the thought—in this heat and humidity it would be like living in an oven.

The truck pulled up, the young soldiers spilled out of the cabin, yelling orders or admonitions at each other and the children who'd run behind the truck. Standing up cautiously, because the kinks had settled back into his spine, Nik stretched, then dropped down to the ground.

They'd stopped outside a building that must originally have been the mine manager's residence. It was a substantial size and had a small office attached to one side. The fact that the soldiers were unloading the truck and stacking boxes on the veranda of the house provided another clue, but no one issued forth to greet the new arrivals.

Nik found Arwon, who seemed to be in charge.

'Is this where the other volunteers are? Frank Butler? The nurses?'

'Frank Butler go,' Arwon told him. 'Plane came in and took him off.'

'"Plane came and took him off"?' Nik repeated. It didn't make any sense at all. 'But we came in on the plane—on the first trip it's made since it brought the others in two weeks ago.'

'Small plane,' Arwon said. 'Frank Butler very sick.'

'From holes made by bullets?' Jack murmured, but Arwon either didn't hear or chose to ignore him.

'The nurse woman makes orders,' Arwon continued. 'She's set up hospital over there.'

He pointed towards a long, low building which had, Nik guessed, been single men's quarters for the expatriate miners who'd been flown in and out on nine-day rosters.

Puzzled by the 'set up hospital' scenario—KidCare's primary aim was to provide services to children and Nik had intended working from the abandoned hospital in the village—Nik left Jack to supervise the unloading and headed towards the building. All the doors and windows were open—no doubt the island had experienced power problems since the departure of the mining company, and air-conditioning was a thing of the past.

He took the two steps up into the building in one stride, landing in a corridor that ran along the right-hand side. Peering into the first room on the left, he saw a woman nursing a baby; the next room had two men, one young and clad mostly in bandages, the other so ancient and still

Nik wondered if he might be dead. In the third room he found someone he knew.

'Paul! What's going on here? What happened to Frank? And why this hospital set-up?'

The solidly built nurse patted the patient he'd been tending reassuringly on the hand, then left the room, taking Nik's arm and leading him out as well.

'Ah, Nik. Welcome to Erireka! Let's talk in the shade outside. The fans we've managed to scavenge stir the air but I don't think it makes much difference to the actual temperature. At least outside you sometimes get a breeze, or, with luck, it might rain on you.'

They'd reached the far end of the building by now, and Paul steered Nik out the door to where some plastic chairs and tables had been set up in the deep shadow of a spreading poinciana tree.

Nik sat, though every fibre in his being wanted to be inside, seeing patients, doing what he knew best—practising medicine. He'd had enough administrative hassles in the last few weeks to last him a lifetime, and had thought coming to Erireka would at least get him away from that aspect of his life.

'Frank Butler had a heart attack. Fortunately, a doctor he knew had taken delivery of a new light aircraft in the US and was flying it out to Australia. He'd arranged to call in and see Frank in Erireka and by sheer good fortune arrived the same day. We stabilised Frank, and his mate, Noel, flew him to Port Moresby. Haven't heard how he's doing, but the radio only works when it wants to, so that's not surprising.'

'When was this?'

Paul scratched his head.

'A week—ten days? Not long after we arrived. It's all a bit of a blur. For a start, the small hospital in town was burnt to the ground when fighting broke out again a few days before we arrived. According to the locals, the rebels did it, but who knows? The local nurse who'd carried on running it after the mining company left was then drafted into the so-called official army, which is why I wonder if perhaps they were responsible for the fire.'

'So there are no medical facilities in the town?' Nik was wondering just how outdated his information was.

'There's very little town,' Paul told him. 'It can't have been big to begin with—hospital, school, church, government buildings and a meeting hall, all built by the mining company, plus a medley of shops. All the buildings the company put up were set ablaze on the same night, presumably to cleanse the island of the scourge of the invaders.'

'So who's in charge?'

'Who knows?' Paul shrugged. 'We deal with a chap called Arwon—you would have met him at the airfield. He belongs to the group who control this area, but how far his power extends, I've no idea.'

Nik nodded. Although, from his information, the fighting in Erireka had ceased well before the team's arrival, and an interim government had been set up, he'd been in similar situations often enough to know you accepted the protection of whoever was offering it.

'So, you've set up a hospital here,' he said to Paul. 'Was it necessary?'

'I wish it hadn't been,' Paul responded. 'But there's been an outbreak of chickenpox, not only in the camp but in other villages, and people have been coming to us—treating us as they would have the local hospital.'

'So we can have patients from both sides of the fighting in the same room?' Nik smiled as he spoke, but it was a grim effort. It wasn't such an unusual situation. Even in refugee camps, he'd seen three- and four-year-old boys carrying on the war of their fathers.

'I suppose we do, but I've no idea what the fighting's about, let alone which side is which. We had a baby brought in yesterday—raging fever, so dehydrated she looked skeletal—and when Ellie asked the mother why she hadn't come earlier, she said because her husband wouldn't let her. We were on the side of their enemies.'

Nik sighed. He'd seen it too often to be surprised, but couldn't fail to be affected.

'The baby?' he asked.

'The baby died this morning. Ellie worked on her all night, feeding her sips of water—'

'Feeding her sips of water? Why not IV fluids? All the necessary equipment was included in the original supplies.'

'She was flat, Nik, barely six months old, and covered with chickenpox vesicles, most of them infected. We couldn't find a usable vein and we didn't have an intraosseous needle to put in an IO line. She could swallow, and Ellie fed her fluid, squirting it into her mouth.'

'Where's Ellie now?'

Paul shrugged.

'Burying the baby, I'd say.'

'Burying the baby? Ellie's burying the baby? And you let her? You and the rest of the crew?'

Nik shot out of the chair, then realised he had no idea where to look for her, and slumped back into it, only half hearing—but fully understanding—Paul's explanation.

'What could we do? You know Ellie once she takes on something. She took on that baby and lost the battle to save its life. Do you think any of us could have stopped her doing what she's doing now?'

'Bloody stubborn woman!' Nik swore, unconsciously choosing her favourite emphasis. 'No, of course you couldn't. But of all people, she's the last one who should be burying babies.'

Even as he said it, he recognised the mistake, betraying a confidence he knew Ellie had entrusted only to him, but fortunately Paul's attention was diverted by a small boy kicking a football at his head, and the moment passed.

But Nik's heart was heavy as he imagined how Ellie must be feeling, and he stood up again, determined to find her and at least offer his physical presence as support.

'Here she is now,' Paul said, and Nik realised he'd been looking in the wrong direction. Turning, he saw a tall, slim, upright woman striding towards him, but this figure, clad in khaki shorts and a faded singlet top, didn't look at all like the Ellie he'd known before. It took him a moment to realise why. The long plait of dark hair that had always swung down the middle of her back was gone—in fact, all her hair was gone, except for a dark sheen of very new growth that clung like a tight cap to a very shapely head.

Fascinated by this change in her, he stood and watched her walk towards him, seeing her face with its thin nose and wide full mouth come into focus, then her steady grey eyes, somehow appearing larger with the lack of hair, met his and he felt a shifting in his chest, as if his heart had somehow expanded and was now squeezing against his lungs, making breathing difficult.

'You look like hell!' she greeted him, holding out her hand to shake his, then tilting her head to one side while she examined him more closely. 'Means you'll fit right in. Has Paul explained?'

Nik grasped her hand and held it for way too long, but something he didn't understand was happening inside him. It couldn't be attraction—he'd set that aside years ago. On top of which, she was almost totally bald, she'd just told him he look like hell, and the one rule he'd tried to be strict about with KidCare missions was the 'no fraternisation among the team' one.

She'd retrieved her hand, though not immediately, and was standing about two feet in front of him, hands on hips, huge grey eyes only slightly reddened by recent tears. The short-cropped hair revealed two neatly positioned ears, with, unbelievably, slightly pointed tips, so she looked for all the world like a wide-eyed elf. A very tall, wide-eyed elf.

Ellie? Elfin?

No, it wasn't the elfin look that startled him, but something else—something within…

Shock jolted through his body—the shock of recognition, not of the person, but of the 'something else' he couldn't understand, let alone explain.

'It's so good to have you here—such a relief,' she was saying. Could she not feel what was happening between them? 'We may complain about your bossiness, but if ever a place needed a good strong boss…'

Her voice tailed off, as if she'd guessed he wasn't really listening. Or maybe the waves of emotion his body *had* to be generating had finally penetrated her.

She frowned, shook her head, then said softly, just for him, smiling grey eyes emphasising the message, 'It's good to have you here.'

Then, before he could react—or even dismiss all the bits of mushy delight dissolving his brain cells—she turned to Paul.

'Did you finish the baths? The old man said you were in Room Five when Nik arrived. Were you working up or down?'

Maybe he'd imagined the smile in her eyes.

'Working up, but now you're here I'll go and finish them. Frank appointed you his deputy, so it's up to you to show the boss around.' Paul grinned at her as he stood up, then he walked back into the 'hospital' building.

Nik was alone with her.

'Are you OK?' she asked gently, and Nik knew she was asking about his reaction to his father's death. She'd known about it—been in touch—sent flowers even—to him, not the funeral or the family. Only Ellie would have considered such a tribute could be equally as meaningful to a man as it would have been to a woman.

She'd sent them as a friend to a friend, he reminded himself.

Vlaka! He had to get past this weirdness—get his mind on the job. Or at least pretend…

He smiled at her.

'You just told me how I look, so what do you think?'

'I think you've been through hell. I know how much your father meant to you.'

She stepped towards him and put her arms around him, hugging him tightly.

As a friend, his mind said, but he held her close for a minute anyway.

'You didn't need to come,' she reminded him, breaking away with a light kiss on his cheek. 'We could have managed without a doctor for a time and you'd have found a replacement eventually. It's not as if—'

'I needed to come,' Nik interrupted, before she could tell him no one was indispensable. Words he'd used to her often enough when she'd pushed herself to the limits of her endurance and he'd had to order her to rest.

She looked at him for a moment, the clear grey of her eyes darkening as if with memories, then she nodded.

'Of course you did. And now you're here, we'd better get on with it. How much has Paul told you?'

'He explained about the hospital being burnt down and the locals coming here for treatment. Also the chickenpox outbreak. I'd got the message to bring chickenpox vaccine and did, although it seemed a strange request.'

Ellie chuckled.

'I thought it would, but we need it to protect the children not yet affected, and, if there's enough to go around, the adult population as well.'

She hesitated, turning to look out over the ugly quarry the mining company had left behind.

'Did he mention the increase in the number of refugees in the camp?'

'An increase in the number of refugees? We're on an island with a population of, what, twenty thousand, tops? And we've more refugees?'

As she turned back towards him, he saw the clean lines of her profile, and the way the new growth of hair feathered around her face. Renewed desire coiled within him, fired by memories of the feel of her body against his, and he felt a mad urge to taste the generous fullness of her lips…

Lips that were explaining, answering his questions…

'There's more fighting, Nik, and you know as well as I do that where there's fighting there will always be people left homeless and children orphaned. I don't have exact numbers, because more people trickle in each day. We're preparing meals for eighty, and can stretch it to one hundred if necessary. Of these more than half are children, and of the children about three-quarters are orphans, or temporary orphans—their parent or parents fighting on one side or the other, or their families deciding to send them here for safety.'

Nik felt a deep sadness well inside him, dampening desire. He understood only too well what she was telling him. He knew villages in Africa where the children made the long walk to the nearest town every evening so they could sleep without fear of being abducted by guerrillas and forced to fight their friends or family.

Yet something didn't fit…

'But these people have lived in peace for ever,' he protested. 'I understood the departure of the mining company left some people destitute, hence the camp, but the fighting—why is it continuing?'

'We don't know,' Ellie said bluntly, but her voice was distracted, and she was looking not at him but at some point beyond his right shoulder. Surprised by her inattention, he half turned to see if there was something going on.

She was watching two figures in military garb—possibly two of the party from the truck—herding a group of children away from one of the shipping containers.

As the kids didn't seem to be in any danger, Nik turned back to his colleague. Her eyes were mesmerising, set, as they were, behind thick sooty lashes and framed by neatly arched eyebrows. He remembered those same eyes, all he had seen of her scarf-wrapped face, studying him intently—sizing him up—the first time they'd met. He'd been mesmerised then, too, for all the good it had done him.

But this time something was different about Ellie—something more than her lack of hair. He couldn't put his finger on it, but he knew it was connected to the jolt he'd felt earlier. To the coil of desire…

Refusing to give his reactions any further consideration, he forced his mind back to the conversation and found the bit that had jarred as she'd said it.

'Eighty meals—we can manage that?'

She nodded, still not looking at him.

'The mining company must have departed in a hurry because they left well-stocked pantries. I imagine their freezers were also stacked with goodies, but the power supply isn't what you'd call reliable, so all that remained in them was a stinking mess. But we do have a good supply of tinned fruit and vegetables, enough to feed this lot for months, plus flour, sugar—all the staples. As for the kitchens, well, Ben's in his element.'

'So, you've about eighty refugees living here in the camp?' Nik was trying to get things straight in his head, but he was also hoping, eventually, to divert Ellie's full attention back to himself.

'No, no.' She answered easily, but her eyes were still on the action beyond him. He could have been a lamppost for all the notice she was taking of him. Though that was nothing new! 'Probably more like a hundred and fifty. But many of them are self-sufficient. They're living here because their homes are no longer safe. The fighters in the hills come down and take the youths away to join them—even the so-called good guys conscript by force. Boys as young as ten have been taken, so families shift in here.'

'And you don't feed them? Surely if the mining company left all that food and we brought in more—I know we did—we can spare something for all of them?'

Ellie shook her head, momentarily diverted from the soldiers' behaviour to look directly at Nik as she explained.

'It's their choice, not ours. Most of these families live on the far side of the mine site, on land that is still in its natural state. They've built their own shelters, brought their livestock with them, have planted crops and go back to their villages during the day to tend whatever they have growing back there.'

One part of his brain took it all in, while the other studied the woman in front of him, wondering if jet-lag could have the effect of stimulating his libido, which would explain why his feelings of attraction to a tall, elfin creature with beautiful, beautiful eyes had suddenly come flooding back.

He'd got over that, and had become a good friend—and had been accepted as *her* friend, mainly, he guessed, because he didn't come on to her.

She was talking about the children now—something to do with schooling—but he'd stopped listening to concentrate on his own problem.

He closed his eyes, thinking that not seeing this particular woman might straighten things out in his head, and when he opened them again, he didn't see her.

She was gone.

CHAPTER TWO

FOR one very small but hopeful moment, Nik thought he might have imagined their entire reunion scene, but furious cries made him turn to see her sprinting towards the two uniformed figures, waving her arms and yelling all manner of dire and bloodthirsty threats.

Nik followed, though more slowly, so he wasn't close enough to protect Ellie when one of the soldiers swung his rifle, catching her across the side of the face with the butt and sending her reeling backwards onto the ground.

He reached her seconds later, scooping her up in his arms, but she fought and struggled like a wildcat, shoving at him, yelling, telling him to let her go.

'Get the boys! They're taking two of our boys.'

He set her down against the container but when he tried to examine the split skin on the red weal rising on her cheek, she pushed him away.

'*Get the boys,*' she repeated, so urgently he knew he had to act.

But, looking around, he found the children and the soldiers had disappeared, though one small child, crying between two containers because he'd been left behind, pointed the way.

He caught up with them in front of the main building and recognised the truck as the one he and Jack had travelled in.

'Leave those children,' he ordered, as two men were attempting to throw a struggling lad into the back of the vehicle, while the second boy kicked and scratched his captor. The younger children stood around, shouting what Nik took to be curses but which could as easily have been encouragement for all he knew.

No one took the slightest notice of him—or his order—so he forced his way through the onlookers and grabbed the shoulder of the man who held the second boy.

'Let him go!' Nik roared, startling the man into releasing his grip. The lad scooted off, and Nik turned his attention to the second captive. 'Him, too,' he said, then recognised Arwon, trying to render himself invisible by the door of the truck.

'Arwon, what's going on here?'

'These men are taking the boys to their fathers. The fathers want sons with them.'

'The boys don't want to go,' Nik pointed out, aware he was treading a dangerously thin line. Care organisations could only operate if they had the support of at least some of the local population. They couldn't afford to be seen as favouring one side over the other, but they needed whoever was in power to provide them with a certain amount of protection.

Arwon regarded him in silence, and Nik knew the man's decision would be pivotal to the success of his venture. But Nik, too, had to stand his ground. Every child deserved a childhood— that was the focal point of the KidCare mission statement—and his head already held too many images of children holding guns.

Then Arwon spoke rapidly to the soldiers, who released the boy. Muttering and throwing black looks at Nik, the soldiers clambered into the cabin of the truck.

'Thank you,' Nik said, bowing slightly to Arwon. 'I hope we can continue to work together for the good of all your people.'

The islander studied Nik a moment longer, then he nodded his head before he, too, climbed into the truck.

It roared away, enveloping all those left behind in a cloud of dust and noxious exhaust fumes.

Nik watched it go, wondering if he'd won or lost the encounter, then felt a tug on his trousers and looked down into the coal-dark eyes of a small girl.

'Sister Ellie, she sick!' the child said.

Hurrying back the way he'd come, he found her, upright, but only because she was holding onto the side of the container, while she kicked up a pile of dirt at the base of it.

'Why didn't you stay sitting where I left you?' he demanded. He slid an arm around her slim waist to support her, anger that she'd been hurt burning inside him when he saw the blood trickling down her cheek.

'I did, then a centipede came along and I had to get up, and I tried to kick it under the container but I think I must have killed it by accident, then I had to cover it up,' she said, looking just as upset over killing a centipede as she had over the boys being abducted. 'I'm all right now. It was the shock earlier that made me a bit woozy. You can let go.'

He did let go, but only so he could swing her into his arms.

'Where's your room?' he asked, but she didn't answer. She just looked at him—eyes wide with an expression he couldn't read.

'What is it? What's the matter?'

She shook her head, and struggled against his grip.

But he knew what it was without her reply. She was feeling what he'd felt on first seeing her earlier today—a sense of recognition so powerful it had resonated throughout his body.

And he knew the next move was inevitable— fated back in some primeval twisting of his genes.

With a stifled moan, he bent his head and kissed her, finding her lips, parted by surprise, easy to access. His tongue explored the soft warm cave of her mouth, tasting honey, flowers, sweet heady wine and, most of all—strangest of all—familiarity.

'Ellie?' he murmured, lifting his lips from hers so he could look at her again—marvelling at what was happening.

She stared up at him, her eyes mirroring the amazement he was feeling, then the smallest hint of a smile danced across her lips, and his mouth was forced to capture them again, in case, in smiling, their taste might have altered.

Ellie eased her lips far enough away from his to enable her, firstly, to breathe and then, as she marshalled her scattered wits, to speak.

'Members of the team are discouraged from developing relationships that go beyond friendship, with either people of the country in which they are guests or with other members of the team. Deeper relationships within an enclosed community such as an aid mission can change the dynamics and disrupt the harmony of the group.'

She looked up into eyes so dark a brown as to appear black as she recited words she knew he had agonised over as he'd written them. But though her voice was calm, her body quivered with an awareness she had never felt before. Nerves tingled, heat suffused her, and it was only with a supreme effort she was able to keep a woozy kind of smile off her lips.

He's stressed out of his mind, jet-lagged from the trip, and picking me up was nothing more than a macho reaction to me being hit, she told herself, concentrating fiercely on why Nik might have been kissing her so that she wouldn't have to consider, firstly, why she'd responded and, secondly, why her body had reacted as it had. Actually, that was secondly, thirdly, fourthly and all the way down to about a hundredly!

'You'd better put me down,' she added, when her words had achieved nothing more than to draw the uncompromising black brows above those arresting eyes into a puzzled frown.

He put her down, but kept an arm around her waist to support her. Then he kissed her again, and she felt warmth this time—a deep, comforting warmth that promised safety as well as excitement. The warmth of home-coming...

Home-coming?

She eased her body from his, desperate to sort out the muddle in her mind, and looked up to find him frowning again.

Though not with anger, she thought—more confusion.

Join the club!

'It took me a long time to work out how to say ''no fraternisation'' without using such an over-worked phrase,' he grumbled gruffly at her. 'But though the rule makes sense, no one ever takes any notice of it. We both know that. Even if it does make sense, because a care team is like a very small community within a community...'

Then he shook his head.

'Why, in the name of heaven, am I telling you this? You were there!'

'Eritrea!' Ellie said softly, glad of the touch of his hand on her arm as she remembered. They'd been in a village miles from anywhere when a group of soldiers had appeared, seizing the villagers' meagre supply of food and locking the aid workers in a subterranean cavern which had once been part of an underground canal system carrying water to the village.

'If I get out,' Nik had said, 'I'm setting up an aid organisation that will focus on kids—on kids being allowed to be kids, on kids being allowed to have childhoods.'

Ellie had understood. The oldest of the 'soldiers' might have been sixteen, the youngest, shorter than the rifle he carried, perhaps five or six.

And because her Aaron had never had the opportunity to have a childhood, she'd known Nik's organisation would be where she'd find a home.

She glanced at Nik, aware of the silence that had stretched between them—knowing where *her* thoughts had been, wondering about his…

'Do you ever get tired of it?' he asked. 'Tired of the uselessness we all feel about a million times a day?' He hesitated, then lifted his hand and ran his thumb down her cheek, before adding in a heart-rendingly gentle voice, 'Tired of burying babies, Ellie?'

Ellie's heart lurched—why wouldn't it? The touch! The voice! The bloody question! But she hid the lurch behind a frown, and blanked the baby from her mind.

Then she rested her hand on his, feeling the need for more contact, as she answered.

'Of course I do. We all do, Nik, you know that. We despair of doing any good. We wonder about the way the world works that the terrible things we see are allowed to happen. But that doesn't mean we should stop—that we shouldn't do whatever we can.'

She smiled at him, hoping to lift the sombre expression on his clean-cut features.

'Did you kiss me because you needed that little pep-talk? Knowing how I'd react to your impromptu advance?'

He half turned, looking out over the abandoned mine, presenting Ellie with a profile that could have been carved on ancient coins.

Ancient coins! Bloody hell! She'd known Nik for years, had even begun to suspect that, beneath the icy armour she'd erected around her emotional self, she might be attracted to him, but she'd never, ever considered his profile. Now here she was, comparing it to something she'd only heard and read about. The baby dying must have thrown her subconscious into disarray—that would explain what she'd felt when

Nik kissed her, and why his profile had suddenly taken on new meaning.

The profile swung her way.

'I kissed you because I couldn't not,' he said quietly.

And Ellie forgot about profiles, too intent on trying to fathom what that reply might mean. Attraction? Well, she'd certainly felt *that*. But why now?

Did why matter?

Did any of this matter? They were here to do a job, not fall in—

Love?

'Do you want to see the kitchens?' She spoke far too abruptly but her meandering thoughts had shocked her to the core, and talking business was the only way she could escape them. 'The cook Frank recruited—you might remember Ben from Afghanistan—has three islanders helping him, and has also organised islanders to help out in the dining room. I know you like to pay any local staff, but when Frank left he was too ill for me to find out how this was to happen, so they haven't been paid. I know you need to see patients, but maybe you could sort this out sooner rather than later.'

'So everyone continues to be fed?' Well-shaped lips spread into a hint of a smile, and

Ellie knew immediately that the kiss had signalled a shift, not so much in the relationship
between herself and Nik but in her life. A tu-
multuous shift! The kiss had caused sensations
in parts of her she'd assumed dead for ever—as
dead as her beloved husband and baby. Now her
body was reacting to that tiny excuse for a smile
and reacting strongly enough for her to suspect
a full-blown smile would have the inner equiv-
alent of a nuclear blast.

Had she felt the same way about Dave's
smile? Had it made her stomach squish with excitement? Start waves of heat in her body? Had
his kisses made her bones melt? Why couldn't
she remember? Questions hammered in her
head, and she prayed her inner confusion wasn't
obvious on the outside.

Grasping desperately at the conversational
opening he'd given her, she managed to blurt
out, 'Exactly!'

And though Nik frowned again, she didn't
think it was because he didn't understand her
answer.

She just hoped it wasn't because I'VE GONE
HAYWIRE OVER NIK was tattooed across her
forehead!

'I think patients first—this hospital you've set
up—then you can show me the kitchens.'

Ellie released the breath she'd been holding. No tattoos! Though the way he spoke the word 'hospital' she guessed they'd shifted into another fairly sticky patch.

'I know we were supposed to be setting up a clinic for mothers and children, and training locals to run it, but— Did Paul tell you about the local hospital?'

'He did.'

'So you understand,' Ellie said hopefully, scanning his face—familiar yet unfamiliar—but not catching a glimmer of understanding. 'We *had* to do something!'

'Of course!'

There was barely a shading of sarcasm in the words, but since the shift in their relationship—oh, stop beating around the bush! Since the kiss!—Ellie had felt super-sensitised and she heard that shading loud and clear.

'Well, we did,' she snapped. 'What were we supposed to do when an elderly man walks the fifteen kilometres out from town with a tropical ulcer that's eaten away half his leg? Tell him we only see women and children? And only women *with* children at that!'

She glared belligerently at the KidCare founder, wanting him to argue, to tell her she was wrong. Wanting, in truth, for things to go back to being as they always had been between them.

But all he did was nod, then he reached out and touched her shoulder. At any other time Ellie would have taken the gesture as confirmation of the nod, a 'you did the right thing' kind of touch, but now her body reacted too convulsively for her to do anything but panic over it—panic and back away. Hastily!

'The hospital,' he reminded her, and she managed to turn her startled movement into a turn in the direction of the hospital.

Walking briskly towards it, she explained, 'Originally each of the rooms was intended for a single mine worker, but we found beds in other buildings and brought them in, so each room holds two patients. There's another similar building and I've been gathering beds for it because I think the chickenpox outbreak is going to get worse and I'd like to separate those patients from the others.'

Nik followed her in through the door, noticing the way she moved—with a little swaying motion of her backside that was as provocative as hell but which, he knew for sure, was as natural to her as breathing. So why had he never noticed it before? Even during his initial attraction to her?

Because of the reserve she'd always worn like a suit of armour? The coolness she projected to hide the depths of her pain and loss and heart-ache?

No, it was more than that. Perhaps it was be-cause she seemed totally unaware of her own beauty, and being unaware of it did nothing to enhance it or show it off.

Though he had always noticed her hair. Had even wondered how long it would be unbound, and if she'd kept growing it as some kind of tribute to her dead husband.

He glanced at the neat cap of new hair on the beautifully shaped head in front of him, and felt a squeezing in his chest that could possibly be asthma—late onset asthma—because he shouldn't be feeling a physical reaction to the thought that maybe Ellie had shaved her head because she'd moved on.

Finished mourning her husband and baby, and found a new love…

Maybe it was a heart attack, this squeezing going on in his chest. He'd been under a lot of stress lately.

He shook his head at the stupid way his thoughts were wandering. He'd learn the para-graph she'd recited at him about no fraternisation and keep repeating it to himself. Get back on track.

Though if she had a new love, surely she wouldn't have responded to his kiss. Responded with such fervour...

He realised she was talking to him—something about the chickenpox—and he hauled his mind back into medical mode.

'Is the chickenpox outbreak bad?'

'Among people already weakened by poor nutrition, contaminated water supplies, poor sanitation and no access to vaccines or other medical supplies? Of course it is.'

They were entering the first room, where an island woman sat on one of the two beds, holding a baby to a badly depleted breast. Both the woman and the infant had the blistered skin of chickenpox, the woman across all that was visible of her skin, the baby less badly affected.

'We have the baby on formula and he's improving—gaining weight, irritated by the rash but otherwise doing fine. But his mother...'

Nik looked at the emaciated woman, who was staring sightlessly out the window.

'Was there no food here? Was the malnutrition so bad a pregnancy brought her to this stage?'

'She's from the hills,' Ellie said softly, moving into the room and gently removing the now sleeping baby from the woman's arms, setting him down on the other bed and pulling a piece of plywood against the side to prevent him rolling out.

The harmful and tragic effects of war spread like ripples from a stone thrown into a lake, affecting the entire community—the woman's pitiful condition too graphic an example. Nik shook his head at the futility of it all.

But while the woman's state struck deeply into his heart, Ellie was all practical help, doing what had to be done with gentle efficiency. She poured a glass of weak-looking milky substance from a jug, and supported the woman while she sipped at it. The woman's empty eyes told Nik of great suffering, and he guessed that all the nutritional supplements in the world wouldn't turn her back into a totally well woman.

She closed her eyes, and Ellie eased her back onto the bed, checked on the baby, then joined Nik in the doorway.

'She was unconscious when she came in—carried on a litter by her mother and her sister, with the baby wrapped on the sister's back. Frank thought encephalitis, but he was gone before she came out of the coma. It could have resulted in brain damage, or she may have been like this before she became ill. The mother and sister disappeared and no one here seems to know her.'

Nik hesitated. It was so easy to walk into a place and, not knowing the circumstances, appear critical. Nonetheless, he had to ask.

'Might she not improve faster if she wasn't feeding the baby?'

'Of course,' his companion said cheerfully. 'But even take him out of the room and she becomes extremely agitated. She's stayed alive for that baby, and sheer instinct is keeping her going at this stage. We do what we can to keep her comfortable.'

They were at the doorway to the next room now, and, from the dressing on his leg, Nik guessed the elderly man who was stuffing an earthenware pipe with some kind of leaves was the man who'd walked in to the camp with the leg ulcer.

'He's not going to smoke that thing in here, is he?'

'He's going to try,' Ellie told him, moving into the room with a determined stride. She stopped in front of the wrong-doer and spoke rapidly in a language Nik didn't understand.

The old man smiled a gap-toothed smile at her and continued stuffing his pipe. On the other bed, a young fellow, bandaged from neck to waist, appeared to be cheering him on.

'I can guess the leg ulcer, but who's our other patient?' Nik asked, as Ellie confiscated the older man's matches and threw them through the window.

'His name's Nudu. We dug a bullet out of his chest a couple of days ago.'

'We?'

'Paul and I, with a little help from Jazzy and Len. We were going to wait until you got here, but we could see it, and wounds turn septic so quickly. Also, it's not as if the soldiers wear pristine clothing. Nudu was wearing filthy rags, and the bullet would have carried fragments of those rags into the wound.'

She was explaining this as if digging a bullet out of a young soldier was an everyday occurrence. Nik thought back over what he knew of her experience in aid work but couldn't place her in an area where there'd been fighting. Even in Eritrea, where they'd ended up shut in an underground tank of some kind, the 'soldiers' had captured them and looted the village without firing a shot.

But he'd always known she'd turn her hand to anything, and do a wonderful job at whatever she took on. The thought made him feel warm all over—no doubt another manifestation of this renewed attraction vibrating through his body. It had to be tiredness making him think and feel things he hadn't thought or felt about Ellie for years, because on top of the 'no fraternisation' rule was the fact that he had a fiancée back in Greece. A woman he barely knew, admittedly, but one to whom he was irrevocably joined.

Or almost irrevocably!

Definitely irrevocably if he wanted to continue the work which had become his passion—this kind of work…

Ellie knew she'd lost him, but he looked more perturbed than angry so presumably they'd done the right thing, digging the bullet out of Nudu's chest. Grabbing a second box of matches from the old man, so he couldn't light his malodorous pipe, she led the way to the next room. The sight of the empty bed re-awoke the deep sadness she'd felt at the death of the baby, but she wasn't going to cry again—particularly not in front of Nik—though as she blinked back a few wayward tears she knew he'd seen them.

She moved determinedly away from the compassionate touch of his hand and introduced him to the little girl in the other bed, the child they called Josie, as near an approximation of her native name as the European workers could manage.

'How long has she been like this?'

Nik squatted by the bed, reaching out to touch the child's face, turning her head so he could see the misshapen skull.

'The mother says always—she was born this way. Not comatose, but with some swelling of the head. At least, that's what Jazzy and I gleaned from the mother. Jazzy—Jasmine—is from New Guinea and though the Erirekan language is different, it has enough in common for Jazzy to communicate with the locals far better than I can.'

Ellie paused, then asked what she and the other nurses had wondered about.

'Hydrocephalus?'

'She's what? Three? Four?'

Practical, medical questions, but practicality didn't dispel the quiver of excitement his voice now generated in her newly sensitive body. But, quiver of excitement or not, she was a nurse first.

'From our calculations, four, though age is a fairly haphazard approximation here. They go by the rains—and she was born four rains ago so maybe even five.'

'And the mother says she was born this way? A newborn with untreated hydrocephalus will rarely survive the neonatal stage. Later onset is known but the unilateral swelling is wrong. So's the position of the swelling, here around the cerebellum.'

His voice, betraying more of his North American background than his Greek origins, was deep but soft, his fingers sure and gentle as he touched the child.

'A tumour of some kind?' Ellie guessed again, while Nik produced a slim pencil torch from his top pocket and shone it, first in the left, then in the right eye of the comatose girl.

'What have you been doing for her?'

'We've done very little, apart from the parenteral fluid dripping into her. Diuretics as well in an attempt to reduce the swelling. She was brought in yesterday. Apparently she had a seizure then didn't recover consciousness. She'd had seizures before, we gathered, but came out of them after a very short time.'

'It's probably all we can do,' he said, a hint of frustration now in the deep voice. 'There's a basic portable X-ray machine in the gear being unpacked now, but I doubt an X-ray will tell us much and we need to ration the film. To me, it looks like a medulloblastoma—a tumour arising in the cerebellum. It's sensitive to radiotherapy but so fast growing that treatment rarely prolongs life more than a year or two.'

Although Ellie had been aware Josie could have a tumour, this confirmation hit her like a physical blow. Surely they couldn't lose two children in such quick succession?

Weren't they here to save children's lives?

'We can't operate?'

'No, we can't,' Nik said gruffly, straightening up and walking out of the room.

'What about radiation? Couldn't we send her to Australia for treatment?'

Ellie followed him out and he spun towards her, pleased to be able to vent a little of the frustration he'd been feeling since he'd seen her eyes fill with tears when she'd walked into the room earlier.

'Put her through that trauma in a strange country to give her two more years? Give her family hope, only to snatch it away? I don't think so.' His frustration oozed away, replaced by a desire to do anything to save this woman more emotional pain. 'We do what we can, Ellie,' he added gently, 'but we're not miracle workers.'

But his words to Ellie didn't soothe his own disappointment, because by coming here—bringing a team here—he'd set up hope. Now, for one family at least, that hope would be dashed away.

And clear grey eyes, meant only to smile, would once again fill with tears...

He entered the next room, aware Ellie hadn't followed—almost as aware of her absence as he had been of her presence since they'd met again.

This was bad.

'Hello!'

The greeting startled him out of his muddled preoccupation. A small boy was sitting up on one of the beds, his broad smile dazzlingly bright against his dark skin.

'Hello!' Nik responded, surprised to find so young a child speaking such clear English. 'And who are you?'

'Hello,' the boy repeated, and he smiled again. Then he pointed to the child on the other bed, and said, 'Harry.' At least, it sounded like Harry.

Nik turned towards Harry and tried a hello in his direction, but the boy, older than his companion, just scowled.

Nik looked around the room, seeking notes about the two boys. None visible—and Ellie had obviously abandoned him.

He was about to go and find her when the 'hello' boy spoke again.

'Ellie loves you,' he announced, as clearly as he'd enunciated 'hello'.

'Ellie loves me?' Nik repeated, drawn against his will into this bizarre conversation.

'No, Ellie loves Patrick,' a female voice said, and Nik turned to find she'd returned, holding in one hand the old man's pipe, which was both dripping water and smouldering. 'I know smoking probably wouldn't do him any harm but I can't let him smoke it inside. I think the leaves contain some form of narcotic because he drops off to sleep and he's already set fire to the bed a couple of times.'

She was waving the pipe in the air as she offered Nik this explanation, adding, 'I smelt it and went back. But I see you've already met Patrick. That's not his islander name, but we call him that. Patrick the parrot. He's a brilliant mimic—hears a word or phrase a few times then repeats it back to you. It makes for some very frustrating conversations.'

'You don't say!' Nik muttered, as the infuriating woman, far from explaining why the two boys were in hospital, whisked off in the direction of the far door, no doubt to destroy the old man's pipe. He followed her into the corridor, and was wondering whether to continue without her when she reappeared, still holding the pipe, and came towards him.

'I don't suppose you brought any pipe tobacco with you,' she said, as if continuing a conversation they'd been having. 'If I could get him something else to smoke—something that didn't make him fall asleep—I wouldn't have to keep worrying.'

'Except about his lung cancer,' Nik said, and she cocked her head towards him and teased him with a smile.

'Was that sarcasm I heard in your voice, Dr Conias?' she asked, then before Nik could reply she added, 'I guess the answer's no—no pipe tobacco. Ah well, he'll just have to suffer. Shall we do the boys next? You've met Patrick. Did he introduce you to Harry? They've both had bad parasite infestations, and suffered from malnutrition as a result. We used drugs to treat the infestation—in them and in a lot of the children we've seen in the clinic—but these two are showing signs of lung involvement—sweating, chills, productive cough.'

'You think the parasites could have reached the lungs?'

Ellie shrugged.

'We've been rather hoping it might be a simple lung infection as a result of their general debility,' she said. 'But they've been on penicillin for two days with little change so, yes, that's probably what's happened. Your X-ray machine will tell you more, but it's bad, isn't it? If the parasites have moved in there.'

She looked at him, the clear grey eyes pleading for him to deny her assumption, as if by some miracle of remote diagnosis, he could allay her fears for the two boys.

So many expectations of him, yet so much he couldn't do!

The woman he knew, but didn't know in this new guise, stood patiently in front of him, head cocked as if she was listening to his thoughts.

Or maybe she was hearing the hum of electricity that flowed between them—a force no amount of inner frustration could diminish.

'If the lung infection was caused by a parasite then it's likely an abscess has formed, and, like any abscess, it needs to be drained before the antibiotics can work. We'll try that. Did you check their teeth?'

'You mean like with horses? To see how old they are?'

She didn't smile but a sparkle in her eyes told him she was teasing him again. Maybe she *had* been listening to his thoughts and was trying to lighten them, but teasing smiles only made his internal combustion problems worse.

'To see if tooth infection might be the source of the lung infection.' The words grated from his lips. 'No point in fixing the lungs if rotten teeth will immediately re-infect them.'

'Len's been doing teeth,' she said. 'He and Jazzy have been running the clinic in town while Paul and I do the hospital. We set up the clinic where the hospital used to be. We used that position because the people had become used to going there if they needed medical attention.'

Nik felt his eyebrows practically knitting themselves together as the implications of this new information successfully pushed thoughts of attraction aside.

'You've two nurses running the clinic in town, leaving only two of you at the hospital? What do you do at night? Who covers night duty?'

'I do nights, and Paul does days, and on days when there's no clinic in town, Jazzy or Len does nights.'

'It's day now and you're here,' Nik pointed out, and Ellie flashed him a radiant smile.

'Well done you!' she said. 'I'll be sleeping later in the day, but it seemed, with Frank gone, the least I could do was stay up to greet you.'

She was lying and he knew it because, for the first time, she failed to meet his eyes.

'You stayed up with the sick baby, not to greet me,' he said, wondering why he felt constrained to point this out—to argue with her.

Because of the attraction?

She shrugged, a gesture he could have interpreted as response to his silent query.

'Maybe a little of both,' she admitted, her voice so low and full of hurt it was all Nik could do not to take her in his arms again.

He was reminding himself of the inherent danger of such a move when her mood shifted again, and she led the way back into the boys' room.

'Come on,' she said to him. 'These two have been waiting long enough.'

Ellie wasn't sure how her behaviour was coming across to her colleague. It was certainly confusing her. She was answering him back, teasing him, switching subjects when she didn't want to answer something he asked, and generally giving the impression of an airhead.

Because he'd kissed her?

Could a kiss cause chaos in the mind as well as tides of sensation through her body?

She led him into the room and watched him examine the two boys, and pulled their notes from under the end of the mattresses to show him.

'Scared they'll read their own notes?' he asked, as he took them.

'Scared the old man will take them to smoke the paper,' she explained. 'It makes the leaves he gets from somewhere—I think one of the soldiers smuggles them in to him—go further, but of course it burns with more flame, hence more potential danger to the bedding, and possibly the entire hospital.'

'You call him ''the old man''? Does he have a name?'

'That *is* his name. In Erirekan it's about a kilometre long and unpronounceable, so we stick to the English version.'

Nik was reading through the notes on the boys as she explained this, and looked up as he finished, the dark eyes seeming to see right into the soft—and at the moment panicky—centre of her being.

Warm dark eyes, sending messages at odds with the businesslike attitude he was adopting.

Though maybe that was her imagination…

'You have power here?'

'Power? As in influence? None at all!'

'Power as in electricity.' Maybe the eyes weren't warm at all!

And she was definitely becoming an airhead.

'The mine had a number of solar cells and although the rebels tried to make off with the storage batteries, they were too heavy. Carl, our general helper, has reattached everything and got the batteries providing enough power to keep the refrigerators running. We run the generator for a few hours every night for lights and to top up the batteries. Will the X-ray machine use much power? If it does, we could run the generator while you use it.'

Ellie was about to congratulate herself on managing this extraordinary situation, with attraction tugging constantly at her senses, quite well—for an airhead—when Nik moved and his arm brushed against hers, electrifying all the nerve-endings in her skin into immediate goosebumps.

'This will go away, won't it?' She was rubbing furiously at her arms and her voice was pathetically faint.

But he must have heard, for he murmured, 'One would hope so!' Then he gave his own arms a rub before telling her about the power requirements of the X-ray machine.

She tried to listen, she really, really did, but for a woman who had, for the last eight of her thirty-four years, denied the existence of physical attraction, what she was experiencing now was mighty scary.

To be experiencing it with Nik was even scarier. If ever a man was way out of her league...

CHAPTER THREE

SOMEHOW she got through the rest of the rooms, three of them, all with chickenpox victims.

'Now, do you want to X-ray Harry's and Patrick's chests or will you take a quick look at the kitchen?'

They were standing outside the building, under the poinciana tree where he'd been with Paul earlier. He studied her for a moment and Ellie, mesmerised by the intensity of his gaze, wondered if those dark eyes could see into her heart and soul.

She sincerely hoped not. Mass confusion reigned in both places.

'You're keen for me to see the kitchen?'

Maybe he'd only been looking into her mind. She smiled at him.

'I am, because it's just about lunchtime, and while you're seeing the kitchen I can start carrying meals over to the patients.' She paused then had to ask. 'Now, why has that made you frown again?'

'Are you doing everything in this place? I may have been distracted during the preparatory phase of this mission but I did keep an eye on the make-up of the team. We had two spare men for odd jobs around the place—Ben to cook and two others. Those two other should be doing things like carrying meals. Who carries them if you're sleeping?'

She shrugged off his concern.

'I get up and help at lunchtime. Paul and I do the meals together, and Ben has been training some local staff, but with all the refugees to feed he needs all the help he can get in the kitchen and dining room. At the moment I help Paul with breakfast before I go off duty, then Jazzy and Len are home in time to do dinner. If Carl's not busy, he helps, but most of the time he's flat out keeping things running or scavenging for parts for his machines.'

Nik couldn't have liked this explanation, for the black brows drew together into a masterly scowl.

'Are you deliberately avoiding answering my question? About the second helper?'

He sounded more stern than cross—the boss wanting answers. But she knew he wasn't going to like the news about Rani, so she tried diversionary tactics—beginning with what she hoped was a distracting smile.

'The answer's yes,' she said, beaming good-will his way.

'What answer's yes?' he demanded. 'Yes isn't what I wanted to hear, Ellie—yes isn't an answer.'

'Yes, it is. It's a yes for, yes, I'm deliberately avoiding answering your question,' she said, her knees a little shaky at her temerity but her voice as level and unconcerned as she could manage.

He looked puzzled by her response but rallied quickly, coming up with an abrupt 'Why?'

A little word, but the way it was uttered warned her not to push him further.

She sighed, and shook her head, then met his eyes.

'There's a possibility Frank wasn't well when he put the team together. Given his heart attack so soon after he arrived, perhaps he was under stress before we left. I'm not blaming him or you or anyone. Obviously, for a mission in this South Pacific region, it was more sensible to get volunteers from Australia and New Zealand, and far cheaper to transport us from there to Erireka.'

'You're deviating again.'

The eyes delivered the same stern message, studying her as if to read any small untruth she might try.

'Not really. I'm explaining why Frank might not have gone into enough detail in recruiting the other member of the team. Rani, the second helper, was Erirekan, and Frank was delighted to get him, particularly as he was willing to spend time with team members before we departed, teaching us some of the basic phrases of his language.'

'And?'

It had to come out, and though she was trying not to sound defensive she knew she probably did.

'He left us when he got here. It turned out he wanted to come back to the island and joining up with KidCare was a convenient way of getting here.'

'For free!' Nik grumbled. 'Where is he now? In the village? Surely if I speak to him, he'd be willing to do something to help his own people.'

'Oh, he's doing that,' Ellie responded. 'Only they're not the same people we thought he'd be helping—or maybe they are, because we don't differentiate between groups when we're providing service, so really we can't hold that against him.'

'Hold what against him?'

Before Ellie could answer, Nik had worked it out for himself.

'He's with the rebels? He headed for the hills?'

The disbelief in the words made Ellie smile, though she knew it was generated more by apprehension than by amusement.

'He's actually their leader—the rebel leader.' She gave the team boss a minute to absorb this before adding the final blow. 'He'd been exiled by the lot who took over after the mine company left. We brought him back!'

She'd never heard anyone swear in Greek before, not even Nik, though she'd seen him angry at times, but it was a pretty safe assumption the flow of incomprehensible language she was hearing was made up of prime Greek swear words.

Nik turned away from the bearer of bad tidings, afraid he'd vent his anger on her. None of it was her fault, and though he felt inclined to blame her for the attraction he was feeling he could hardly blame her for this man's duplicity and defection.

Neither could he wonder how this had happened. Had he been doing the recruiting, he'd have been delighted to find a native Erirekan willing to volunteer.

But the rebel leader?

He swung back towards Ellie.

She was standing there, as if waiting for him to get over his snit and ask more questions, which he intended doing. Except just looking at her made him forget his anger because all he could remember was how her kiss had tasted.

Honey—he was sure he'd tasted honey...

'You're wondering how we stand with the local militia after bringing back the leader of their enemies,' she said, and he was startled to realise she was right. That was exactly what he probably should have been wondering—would have been wondering if he hadn't been thinking about honeyed kisses...

'So where *do* we stand?'

She waggled her hand back and forth.

'We're taking it day by day. So far, apart from the episode this morning when the soldiers tried to take the boys, we seem to be getting on all right, but I've told all the staff to stay alert. I believe while the locals we've recruited to help in the clinic in town and in the kitchen turn up each day to work, we're OK. But if it happens that one day none of them turn up, I think we'd be in trouble.'

'You seem remarkably calm about all this,' Nik said, though he remembered how Ellie's magnificent composure had got them through other tight places and wondered why he'd never been so struck by it before.

'What do you expect me to do? Run around in a panic? That won't help anyone. Cry?'

She stared defiantly into his eyes.

'I only cry for children—never for myself. You should know that, Nik.'

The fierceness he'd heard in her voice earlier was back—and he knew she spoke the truth. The Ellie he knew was definitely not a woman who indulged in self-pity.

But this wasn't the Ellie he knew! This was an elfin creature who'd cast some kind of spell over him. A spell strong enough to have the air between them quivering with tension.

He reached out towards her, drawn by something he couldn't explain, and for a moment thought she was going to move into his arms. Then she touched his hand as if to acknowledge what was going on between them and turned away, leading him towards the kitchen.

A steady stream of people was moving in the same direction—seemingly too many for one cook to feed.

'*How* many helpers does the cook have?' he asked.

Ellie turned back towards him, pleased whatever it was that had passed between them seconds earlier seemed safely behind them.

'Four or five regulars who work with him in
the kitchen. Some of the older children also help
with the serving of meals. They'd be willing to
carry meals to the hospital, too, but I don't want
them mixing with the chickenpox victims.'

'But there must be chickenpox victims not in
hospital. They could be mixing with them.'

'Yes, but if they catch it outside, it's different.' She stopped walking so she could look at
him as she explained. 'I can't help feeling we'd
be somehow to blame—or could be seen to be
to blame—if they could point to contact with
hospital patients as the source of their infection.
Arwon would have let us have some of his men
to help in the hospital, but...'

Ellie couldn't go on—unable to put into
words her strong presentiment that it would take
very little for the soldiers to turn against them.

'But you don't trust them?' Nik reached out
and touched her chin, and with the barest of
pressures turned her face so she was forced to
look at him, not at a distant point beyond his
shoulder.

She shrugged at the discomfort both his touch and the question caused, though the discomfort was trickier than the question.

'It's not lack of trust so much as a general uneasiness. There's a constant feeling that we're treading on eggshells here. As if one false move, one unfortunate remark, could turn these so-called allies into enemies.'

'Are Paul and the other staff as worried over this as you are?'

'Probably not,' Ellie replied honestly. 'Paul takes things very much as they come. Jazzy and Len, because they're working in the town, see less of the soldiers, who tend to hang around the camp. And because they're working in town, they're building up a network of support among the locals there, so they kind of have their own protection. I guess they're more accepted than we are, because we have refugees from both sides in the camp and in the hospital.'

He looked at her for a moment longer but, so aware of him her skin was burning—though maybe that was the tropical sun—Ellie moved away, leading him through the back door into the kitchen.

Ben, their cook, was slicing meat from a huge leg of pork. He was clad in a pair of ragged shorts and a T-shirt that might once have been green but was now a spattered, faded grey. His long hair was pulled back into a ponytail and facial hair obscured most of his features, but in contrast to his looks he was meticulously clean, and one of the best workers Ellie had ever known.

'Ben, you remember Dr Conias?'

'Nik.' Nik held out his hand towards Ben then realised it was hardly the time for hand-shaking. 'You're doing a good job there.'

Ben nodded and kept cutting meat.

'Patient meals ready on that table, Ellie. I did a kind of soup for the baby's mother—thinking you might be able to get her to drink it. Make a change from that protein drink you've been giving her.'

'Thanks, Ben.'

Ellie walked past him to where he'd set out the meals, six to a tray, small printed squares of cardboard with names on showing which meals went where.

'The old man. Nudu. The baby's mother. Patrick and Harry.'

Nik was right behind her, reading out the names. 'You take that tray and I'll test my wait-person skills with two.'

'You don't have to carry meals over,' Ellie protested, but he had moved around her and was already sliding his strong, capable-looking hands under the two trays.

'And you do?' he said, dark eyebrows rising in further interrogation.

Ellie decided it was easier to ignore this question—easier to pick up her tray and walk away. She could feed the baby's mother the soup Ben had made, which would keep her out of Nik's way while he gave out the other meals. After which she was overdue for a sleep. It could be tomorrow before she had to face Nik again.

Before she had to battle the strange reactions within her body his presence generated...

Nik lifted the trays and followed her out of the kitchen. He'd take the meals across to the hospital, leave Paul to handle things from there and go back to the house to see how the unpacking was progressing. He needed to X-ray the boys' chests, visit the clinic in town...

How?

He lengthened his stride to catch up with Ellie—a good idea, given the way he'd been watching her hips sway as he planned his afternoon.

'What transport do we have? Did Frank manage to buy some vehicles before he took ill?'

She seemed unsurprised by his question, glancing over her shoulder towards him as she made her way up the steps into the makeshift hospital.

'He tried, but there wasn't anything available. The so-called army had acquired all the mine vehicles. At first, one of the boys drove Jazzy and Len into town each morning and brought them back in the afternoon, but this week Arwon's allowed them to take a car. Len's very good with anything mechanical and he and Carl are quietly fixing up an old wreck they found here at the mine site. The army boys simply abandon any vehicle that stops going. If filling it with fuel doesn't make it go, they leave it where it dies.'

'So if I want to visit the clinic this afternoon, I ask Arwon for a lift.'

She'd stopped outside the woman and baby's room, tray propped against the wall. The shapely head turned towards him, and he saw concern—panic?—in the wide grey eyes.

'Don't go on your own!' she said. 'Not with Arwon or any of the soldiers. Take Paul—I'll stay on the ward. Or Carl if you can find him, or take Ben when he's finished lunch—though he usually starts on dinner as soon as lunch is cleared away.'

It *was* panic—he could hear it in her voice.

'The soldiers can't be trusted?'

Now she looked worried, and he was hit by the notion that he didn't want her worrying.

About anything…

'We don't know, and for that reason we made it a rule we'd only leave the camp in pairs. It's a rule in a lot of places.'

'And in many places, if a local group wants to kidnap care workers, they simply take them both.'

She tilted her chin in a gesture he knew from the past was a prelude to an argument.

'It's still a sensible rule,' she said, then she turned away, carrying the tray not into the mother and baby's room but into the room next door, offering plates to the old man and Nudu.

Nik left her to it, walking further down the corridor, then realising he couldn't hand out meals when both his hands held trays. Fortunately, Paul appeared from the room at the far end and took one tray.

'Doing my job?' Paul asked.

'Doing what I can to help,' Nik told him.

'Then I'll book you for the clinic we run here after lunch. It's fairly informal—under the poinciana tree, in fact—but we're getting more people turning up every day. One of the local women who worked in the office at the hospital does the translating and recording for us. Her name's Millie, and according to her, the mining company started a comprehensive immunisation programme and most children had a full course of triple antigen before they started school. But the younger ones—born since the mine closed— have missed out, so we've been immunising them. Some pregnant women come—we've giving them supplementary nutrition through biscuits because their food intake was poor before we arrived. Parasitical infections are common in most of the kids—that, and now, of course, the chickenpox.'

Nik nodded, understanding Paul's outline of the usual clinic patients, but puzzled over the demographics of this camp. There were obviously people still living in the town, or there wouldn't be a need for a clinic there. There were people living in their own makeshift village here within the boundaries of the abandoned mine and yet more people living as refugees—presumably in or around the shipping containers. Where had they come from?

What he needed wasn't to be handing out lunches or taking a clinic under the poinciana tree, but a tour, first of the camp then of the area beyond it—the area they talked about as 'town'.

He left the lunches with Paul and made his way back to the big house where Jack had not only unpacked the X-ray machine but had also managed to find out a lot more about the political situation.

'It's easy,' he told Nik, leading him back towards the kitchen and dining room because, as he'd said, 'If I didn't make sure you ate you'd starve to death.' 'There were about fourteen tribes, I suppose you'd call them, on the island, centred around twelve villages and what they call "the hills". The tribes were loosely related in three main what we might call ethnic groups—the hill people, the lowlanders and the fishermen. The fishermen tribes, naturally, lived along the coast, and traded their fish with the lowlanders for grain and meat. The lowlanders kept pigs and cattle and farmed a bit around their villages, but the hill people lived mainly by hunting and gathering food from the jungle.'

'OK, I've got that,' Nik said, as they entered the dining room.

It had been deserted earlier when he'd looked through from the kitchen, but now every table was occupied, and the mainly women and children talked quietly as they ate their meals. A few islanders circulated among the tables, taking empty plates, serving food to latecomers.

'So, who are this lot?' Nik asked, waving his hand to indicate the throng.

'On the whole they're lowlanders. Seems them and the hill people have always been at odds—the hill people carrying out raids on the lowlanders' stock, the lowlanders cutting back more jungle for their crops. Most of the army— the lot we're working with—are lowlanders, with a few fishermen thrown in—young fellows who like the excitement of being in uniform.'

'And the other fishermen?'

One of the native staff had shown them to a table with two spare seats. Nik nodded to those already seated and sat down.

'They stayed in town. The people here are from the tribes who lived closest to the hills— they were worst off when fighting broke out and the hill people started attacking them all the time, stealing animals, burning crops and housing.'

'And the lowlanders from close to the camp? They're the people Ellie mentioned—the ones who've virtually set up their own village here at the mine?'

Jack nodded, then turned to thank a woman who'd put a plate of cold meat and vegetables in front of him.

'You *have* been getting around,' Nik said admiringly, though he didn't know why he was surprised. Jack always gleaned far more about any place they visited than he himself ever could.

'Didn't waste any time kissing a pretty nurse,' Jack retorted, and Nik felt his cheeks heat at the censure in Jack's voice.

'Not that you kissing the nurse is any of my business,' Jack added, but it was, of course. Jack knew about Lena—knew about the will—and to Jack, KidCare was the most important aspect of Nik's work.

Of his life, probably, Nik thought gloomily. At seventy-five, Jack had probably forgotten all about sexual attraction—if the gloomy old bastard had ever known it!

But Jack was right. KidCare had become a priority and should remain that way, and with the no-fraternisation rule to help him, he was going to beat the inconvenient attraction he felt towards the woman who'd been his friend.

'She does night duty—you don't need to see her.'

Nik stared at the older man.

'Are my thoughts printed in a cartoon bubble over my head?' he demanded.

'No, but I've known you a while now—and you're distracted. Only other time I ever see you distracted—even taking in your father dying and his will and all—was when that skinny redhead had you on a string for a while. Ellie, now, she ain't nothing to look at, not like the redhead, but you got that distracted look in your eyes just the same. You had a bit of a thing for her before, and it didn't do you no good, now, did it?'

Deciding to ignore Jack's percipience, Nik tackled his meal, only realising, as Jack finished and excused himself to do more organising, that he still didn't know who was fighting whom. He guessed the hill people and the lowlanders were at war—but why would the hill people have been bothered by the mine?

'Everyone was bothered by the mine—even the army. It was general dissatisfaction and raids by militant groups that caused the company to pull out.'

Ellie was providing the explanation. Did she never sleep? He'd finished X-raying the boys' chests, and had been dismayed to find Patrick had abscesses in the posterior segments of both left and right lobes, though Harry was luckier, with a small abscess in the right middle lobe. He'd given Paul some instructions for postural drainage, showing him how to position the boys, then had come out to do the clinic. And who should be there but Ellie?

Knowing he needed something to distract him from her presence, he asked the question that had been worrying him.

'So who's fighting who now?'

'Hill people and lowlanders—the lowlanders make up the bulk of the army and while they were away fighting the mine lot, the hill people took back land they claimed was rightfully theirs, land they said the lowlanders had cleared illegally.'

'Ah!' Nik said, as everything became much clearer. In most of the countries in which he'd worked, territorial claims had triggered war. Hadn't most wars throughout history been triggered by the same thing?

'Millie's sick, that's why I'm here.'

He hadn't asked but, having been offered this explanation, he now found he needed to pursue it.

'If you were sleeping—which is what you should be doing right now—how did you know Millie was sick?'

'She came up to the house—high temp, shivering, probably chickenpox starting. I'd rather that than some new disease breaking out.

Anyway, she's been living in one of the shipping containers, and they provide shelter from rain but are terribly hot. We've no more beds in the hospital unless I put her in with Josie, which I really don't want to do, and realistically there's not enough staff to start another separate ward, so I put her to bed in my bed and came down to do the clinic.'

'And you'll sleep when? And where?'

Ellie had been going through a sheaf of papers in a loose-leaf folder as she'd given her explanation, but at his question looked up.

'You're not going to tell me you've never been twenty-four—or even forty-eight hours without sleep. Every new intern—did you study in America or Greece?—does it at some time.'

She watched him, head cocked to one side, as if waiting for an answer to the personal question she'd slid into the conversation.

'Canada. I studied in Canada,' he said, then realised she'd distracted him from what they'd been discussing. Though why she'd be asking this now when she'd known him on and off for years…

Simple distraction, or something else?

Surely not interest!

Nik's heart swelled with hope.

'Ah! That explains the softer accent. I've often wondered about it, you know. It's not entirely American, but not Greek or English or anything much else.'

She smiled at him and it took a huge effort to remember the pact he'd made with himself after lunch. If her aim was to distract him, it was working, though for all the wrong reasons!

'My accent isn't under discussion,' he said sternly. 'Your behaviour is. You're a nurse— you should know you have to look after yourself if you're going to function properly. Letting a sick woman have your bed was hardly sensible. What happens when you catch whatever it is she has?'

Ellie was unaffected by his scolding, grinning blithely at him.

'I've been vaccinated against chickenpox and just about every other pox and infection known to man, and I'm not intending to go to bed with her, you know. I'll find somewhere else to sleep when the clinic's finished, and if I leave a note for Jazzy, she'll cover for me here until I wake up.'

'You've got it all organised, haven't you?' Nik said, feeling testy about the situation yet unable to pinpoint a reason for his reaction.

And she heard it, for she looked at him, her expression genuinely perplexed.

'But it's only how we always work in volunteer situations,' she reminded him, then she smiled again, and he felt all his good intentions melting in the radiant warmth of that expression.

CHAPTER FOUR

'I'M ENGAGED,' he announced some time later, looking up from a tropical ulcer he'd been cleaning.

It wasn't at all what he'd meant to say. He'd meant to ask Ellie for a dressing, but her smile had lingered in his head as they'd treated four patients, and apparently his mind had latched on to making the declaration as a way of banishing the smile.

'To anyone you know?'

Teasing delight glimmered in her eyes as she passed him the dressing he hadn't requested.

'I'm serious,' he growled, and heard her sigh.

'When aren't you?' she said tiredly, then she added, 'Don't mind me. I just seem to have lost the plot today. Put it down to relief that some-one else can now be in charge.'

He secured the dressing and looked up to see all the laughter gone from her eyes, while her usually full lips had tightened into a thin line.

Aware he had caused the light to die out of her face, he tried to find words to explain his abrupt declaration, but she held up a hand.

'Patients to see,' she reminded him, and gestured to a pregnant woman with a toddler hanging on her skirt to come forward.

The woman was emaciated, her swollen belly standing out from a skeletal frame. Ellie was right—there were patients to see. Prioritise, Conias!

Ellie had helped the woman onto a low stretcher, and was taking her blood pressure, talking haltingly in the foreign tongue he'd heard her use earlier. The rebel leader, Rani, had obviously done some good—teaching basic Erirekan to the members of the team.

'She's from a hill village,' Ellie translated for him, though he doubted that was all Ellie had learned, given the woman's rapid-fire conversation and gestures.

'What's been happening that she's in such poor condition? The child looks well fed,' Nik said as he mimed a request for permission then laid his hands over the woman's belly, feeling the hard shape of a foetal bottom tucked high up near her ribs.

'War's been happening,' Ellie said bluntly. 'If I've got it right, her husband either died fighting or left her to go fighting. She was raped by some soldiers—who knows which lot—realised she was pregnant, and decided the baby would die if she didn't eat. Of course, all it did was take the nutrients it needed from her body and now she thinks it's due, she's worried she won't be strong enough to give birth.'

'And *she'll* die,' Nik said softly, the heart he'd thought hardened to this type of thing growing heavy with the pain of human behaviour. Or should that be inhuman behaviour? 'Only she won't, with us to help her. Can you ask her name?'

More rapid fire conversation.

'It sounds like Marnika,' Ellie told him, and when he repeated the word the woman smiled and nodded.

'Will she be willing to stay in the camp until the baby comes?'

Ellie spoke to the woman, who took her hand and nodded, relief lightening her thin face.

'She's worried for the toddler—worried who will care for him if she dies. I think she came in because she realised if she was in the camp he would be looked after.'

'And the baby?' Nik asked quietly. 'How will she feel about it? Will she keep it?'

Ellie looked up and met his eyes—no smile in hers this time, just a plea for understanding.

'I'm not sure I can ask her that,' she murmured. 'Maybe she doesn't know herself, though it's not the baby's fault, is it?'

She hesitated, still looking at him, her eyes giving away her anxiety over the implications of the baby's birth.

'Can we get her well first? Or at least as well as we can manage? Maybe when she's feeling stronger she'll be able to decide what's best.'

Nik felt his chest tighten. This was the Ellie he knew best—caring, practical, sensible and seemingly detached from the emotional storms in which they worked. Yet it was as if he'd never truly appreciated just how special all those qualities were in situations like this.

He wanted to say something—he wasn't sure what. Maybe how much he admired her. But she was busy measuring the fundal height with a small plastic tape measure she'd produced from somewhere about her person.

'I know this is a rough way of measuring gestation if she's gone past thirty-two weeks, but from fundal height she's at least that.'

'More, assuming the baby's small,' Nik said, again feeling the way the foetus was lying, head tucked down in ready-for-business position. 'And as she's come in, we have to assume she knows she's fairly close.'

'Earlier she said she didn't know,' Ellie said, then she turned away, speaking again to the woman. When she looked back at him, there was a world of pain in her eyes. 'I think it might have happened more than once.'

Nik felt his gut tighten. Though he'd seen the results of such barbaric behaviour often enough in other war-torn areas, it was something he could never get used to or accept.

'We'll look after her,' he said, reaching out and touching Ellie's shoulder, then covering the gesture with practicality. 'It might be more acceptable to her if you do the more thorough examination. I'll move on to the next patient.'

Ellie watched him walk away, then she explained to the woman that she'd like to examine her. Dark wary eyes studied her for a moment, before the woman gave permission.

He's engaged, Ellie said to herself as she listened to the baby's heartbeat, strong and steady, then continued the examination, finding the cervix already soft and ripe, even partially effaced.

He's told you that because whatever has been happening between us today can come to nothing.

Not that anything ever could have come of an attraction between us.

Different worlds…

'The baby will come soon,' she suggested to the patient, as her examination, carried out efficiently in spite of her distracted mind, confirmed all was well, apart from the woman's poor condition. 'So we need to make you stronger so you are ready for it.'

She brought out a packet of biscuits and a tin of the protein supplement they mixed with water to make a nutritious drink.

'You will stay with us until the baby comes?' she asked again, not at all sure if she was getting the Erirekan words right.

The woman nodded, and Ellie called to one of the young girls who were playing nearby. The child's mother, Maze, was a natural organiser. She'd find somewhere for the latest arrival to stay, and guide her through the intricacies of camp life.

While they waited for Maze, Ellie explained about mixing the powder. 'I want you to eat meals with all the others, but try to drink a glass of this milk and eat two biscuits between the meals.'

She gave Maze the same advice, asking her to see the woman tried to eat and drink, though Ellie knew she was in such a debilitated state she'd only be able to pick at her food, and would probably find eating even one biscuit a huge effort.

Had she come to them too late? They wouldn't know until labour began and the woman's starved body was put to the test.

Worrying about the woman—and the baby she would soon deliver—and writing up some notes kept Ellie's mind off Nik and his uncharacteristic behaviour.

Off her own uncharacteristic behaviour, too, come to that. Bloody hell! He'd kissed her! Big deal!

But though she tried to tough it out, she knew it wasn't the kiss which had upset her, but her reaction to it—the deep sensual yearning he'd awoken in her body.

If one kiss could do this, what about…

She pushed the notes away and looked around. The cause of her concern—the engaged cause of her concern!—had disappeared, as had the rest of their clinic patients. Perhaps Marnika had been the last but one. Ellie hadn't really noticed, too intent on not noticing Nik and trying to work out why two words—*I'm engaged*—had caused such pain in her chest.

It's tiredness, she told herself, and she made her way up into the hospital building, checking all was well as she passed each room, until she came to the bed where the baby had been. There were clean sheets on it—thanks to the camp women who'd appointed themselves keepers of the laundry.

Ellie checked Josie's drip was running, then sank down onto the empty bed. She'd feel better about everything when she'd had some sleep. Even the kiss business might make sense.

Nik saw her there when he entered the room, intending to carry little Josie up to the house where he'd set up the X-ray machine. Jasmine and Len had returned from the town, and they'd all had dinner together. Now Len was setting up two inclined boards to make the postural drainage easier for Patrick and Harry, while Jasmine was bathing the patients with chickenpox, doing what she could to relieve the irritation of the skin lesions before they slept.

So Ellie could sleep.

And he could watch her.

Greek words he knew but had never used floated through his mind. *Agape mou*—my love; *kyria mou*—my woman.

Madness, that's what it is, practical English told him, but still he watched, torturing himself deliberately with thoughts he shouldn't have, until her eyelids fluttered and he wondered if the tension thrumming through his body was sending pulses across the space between them, battering on her skin.

He turned away, towards Josie, the child Ellie so wanted him to save. Could it be something other than a tumour?

Only in a fairy-tale, reality suggested, but he moved carefully, detaching the drip from the small, limp hand, and gently lifting the frail body into his arms.

Fifteen minutes later he had his fairy-tale. He let out a whoop of delight that echoed through the house.

'Ellie's asleep in the second or third room in the hospital—could you get her for me?' he said to Jack, who'd been acting as X-ray technician for him. 'And Len, who's at the hospital, and Paul, too—I've no idea where he is.'

Jack bustled off, and Nik shifted the little girl from the wooden bench they'd set up as an X-ray table onto a sheet on the floor, so if she did move she couldn't fall. Then he strode through the dwelling he'd only partially explored. The dining room, complete with abandoned dining-room table, would make a fine operating room, though they'd need more light. Carl would have to use the generators.

Ellie arrived, still flushed from sleep, as he was mentally listing what he needed.

'It's not a tumour but an abscess,' he told her, then realised she'd have no idea what he was talking about. 'Little Josie. I'd say it was caused by the same parasite that's infected the boys. I want to drain it—drill a burr hole and insert a drainage tube.'

'Now?'

She glanced at her watch, obviously still be-fuddled by her short sleep. Then she frowned and added, 'Josie?'

But before he could explain again, the frown cleared and a warm, delighted smile spread across her face, giving her skin a luminous look and making her eyes sparkle with hope.

'It's an abscess? You can drain it? You can save her?' She shook her head, then murmured 'Oh, Nik!' so gratefully—so lovingly—his heart stopped beating.

Ellie was so overwhelmed by this unbeliev-able news. It took all her self-control not to throw herself into Nik's arms and hug him.

In gratitude, of course!

Thankfully, the nurse in her took over. 'Where will we do it? What do you need? Do we have the proper equipment or will we have to make do?'

She'd heard and read of burr holes being drilled with a carpenter's brace and bit, but didn't really want to have to search the abandoned mine sheds for such a tool.

'I've got what we'll need, though light's a problem. Carl will have to make sure we've enough power coming from the generator for extra light. I'll get Jack to speak to him and find more lights, if you organise drapes and dressings and set up the instruments on some kind of table or tray. You'll find Jack's unpacked most of the gear we brought with us and has it stacked and labelled in the little office next to this house.'

Ellie hurried away, her mind running through what would be required. Find Carl first—they had to be absolutely certain of the light. Then anaesthetic, and a range of scalpels, retractors, a hollow needle, tubing...

So much to do, but her feet seemed to be moving above the ground, such was her joy in this diagnosis.

'It must be huge to have caused such obvious malformation,' Ellie said. It was barely an hour later and she was gowned, masked and gloved, standing beside Nik as his assistant, holding the retractors, while Paul controlled the anaesthetic, and Len gathered up the swabs and used instruments and generally acted as a gofer. Paul was watching little Josie closely, taking pulse and blood pressure constantly, doing the job a complex monitor would do in a modern operating theatre.

'Surely a small abscess wouldn't deform skull bones.'

Dark eyes slid towards her, the pale blue mask making them seem darker. 'Maybe there *was* a malformation of the skull from birth,' Nik said, picking up the small hand tool he would use to drill the hole. 'The plates of the skull could have been squeezed out of shape during the baby's passage down the birth canal, as sometimes happens, and then didn't, for some reason, go back into their normal position. Didn't you say the mother claimed Josie's head had always been this way?'

Ellie nodded, though her memories of what she might have said and done earlier in the day were fairly vague.

Most of her memories!

'So the abscess was recent, first causing seizures as it pressed on the brain then, as it grew, sending her into a coma?' she guessed.

Nik didn't reply, all his attention on the small hole he was drilling in the skull.

Ellie saw the slight give as the instrument bit through to the membrane beneath the bone and, holding the retractors in one hand, reached out for the little instrument that would hook the membrane through the hole so Nik could cut it.

They were working so close together she could feel each intake of his breath, and although her mind was one hundred per cent focused on what she was doing, another part of her was tensely aware of that physical closeness.

Of the attraction that had come from nowhere—or seemingly nowhere. To be honest, she'd felt it the last time they'd been together, but had assumed it had simply been her body reawakening from long-term grief.

'Hollow needle and suction.'

The demand had her hand moving automatically, passing Nik first the needle he required, then the rubber ball he would fit to it to suction out the debris.

Her mind, seeking distraction from the distraction of attraction, shifted to the state-of-the-art theatres where her young patients had their operations in her other life as a specialist post-op paediatric nurse in a large city hospital. Would the result of this operation be any less successful because of the primitive conditions under which it had been performed? Because there was no electronic suction machine?

'Early surgeons performed operations in far less sterile conditions,' Nik remarked, setting aside the needle and suction bulb and choosing a thin, pliable plastic tube from the selection Ellie had laid out for him.

She glanced at him, and smiled behind her mask, not really surprised to find their thoughts on the same wavelength. It had often happened when they'd worked together in the past, and they'd even discussed it, coming to the conclusion their minds must operate in similar ways and thinking nothing more about it.

Now it was a bit freaky, considering the way her mind kept slipping out of medical gear and thinking things it had never thought before.

Things she'd prefer Nik didn't know she was thinking...

He taped the drainage tube into place and covered the wound.

'She'll need to be monitored closely. Paul, you, Len and Jasmine need to get some sleep, so I'll sit with her tonight. Ellie, you take over your own shift at the hospital from Jasmine.'

'You need sleep, too, Nik. I can watch Josie at the hospital—nights are quiet,' Ellie told him, helping Len clear away the rest of the instruments. They had a basic autoclave, and would put them all through it so they'd be ready for re-use when necessary. There were no luxuries like pre-packed surgical kits here.

'Not quiet enough for you to be there all the time,' Nik said, and though Ellie knew he was guessing, she also knew he was right. 'We've got to be alert for seizures as she comes out of the anaesthetic. They're a possible after-effect of a brain abscess. Once she's stabilised after the op we can look at anti-epileptic drugs for her, but while she's still fragile we'll have to deal with them as they occur, so we'll need to keep diazepam on hand.'

Acknowledging her agreement with a nod, Ellie helped Len clean up, then walked across to the hospital to relieve Jazzy. Nik would bring Josie across when he was satisfied she could be safely moved. She was his concern now.

Josie would live! Gratitude welled in Ellie as she walked along the corridor outside the rooms, peering into each one, using a dimmed torch to check her patients. The mother and baby were both sleeping, the next room empty—though Jazzy or someone had tidied both the beds. The old man was awake and waved to her, then indicated the empty bed beside him.

'He's gone back to fight,' the old man, whose English was better than her Erirekan, told her when she came into the room to make sure Nudu wasn't anywhere in it.

'He's not well enough,' Ellie muttered, but she'd seen it coming. The young man had been getting edgier and edgier, cooped up in bed. Telling herself they'd done all they could for him, and surely he'd already had his share of bad luck, she moved on.

In the next room, Harry was asleep, but Patrick, though dozing, was fidgeting on the inclined board Len had set up for him. Sleeping on it wouldn't be easy, but the angle would help drain the abscesses.

The next option—should they not drain— would be surgery similar to what they'd done on little Josie, though draining an abscess in a lung meant more invasive surgery than a burr hole, and Patrick had abscesses in both lungs.

Poor little boy, Ellie thought, squatting by his bed and stroking his forehead until he settled into a more restful sleep.

Once satisfied he'd stay asleep, she left the room, and saw movement back the way she'd come. Nik, with Josie in his arms.

She turned back so she could use her torchlight to show him into the room, the generators having been turned off as soon as the operation had ended, the main house lights running off the batteries.

Gently, he lowered the quiescent child onto the bed, his hand straying to touch her cheek before he straightened.

'Do these room lights work at night?' he asked, and Ellie shook her head.

'Not once the generator goes off, but I've a lamp I'll bring in. It works on batteries and gives a good light. We found a number of them in a storehouse here on site.'

Nik nodded to her but, though she knew it was a dismissal, she couldn't move away—held in place by some invisible power, strung, like taut wire, between them.

Feelings she'd never expected to experience again—maybe had never experienced before, even with Dave—flooded through her. Deep, warm, undeniably sexual feelings, though no part of her body was in contact with Nik's. In fact, there was a distance of at least a metre between them, and Nik stood as motionless as she was.

Time blurred into eternity as some essence of the man she'd for years thought of as a friend wrapped around her body and crept into secret places too long forgotten—or ignored. And with it came desire—so strong it stole her breath and made her knees tremble uncertainly…

Her face was nothing more than a pale oval in the dim light, yet Nik felt he could see it clearly—see also, mirrored in her stance, the tension he was feeling, bowstring tight, in every sinew of his body.

What was this? It was far too strong to be listed under such a weak word as 'attraction'. Lust?

Why now?

And why Ellie, of all people, whom he'd accepted was off limits and so had turned her into a good friend?

Useless questions staggered about in the confusion of his mind, while his body strained to touch hers—burned to hold her—yet did not move.

'I'm not engaged engaged,' he heard a rough voice say, and knew the nonsense had emanated from his lips.

He tried to make amends.

'It's complicated.'

Good! Voice not quite as hoarsely rugged, though his body was still held in bondage to an unseen force.

'It's not my business,' he heard her breathe, but still she stood until it seemed an eternity had passed, an eternity of awareness, sparking with ruthless intensity between them.

Then she rubbed her free hand across her face and broke the spell, walking away, soft-footed, so it seemed as if it had been a ghost who'd stood there before floating on to other haunts. By the time she returned with the lamp, the incident might never have occurred, though his body was more aware of her presence than it had ever been of any other woman's, and his heart hammered as she leaned close to where he sat on the edge of the bed and adjusted the lamp's light to a steady, yellow glow. The air filled with the delicate, erotic, indefinable smell of her femininity, and the physical manifestations of his reaction were so strong he was forced to speak again—to at least attempt to explain the random messages he'd been delivering.

'My father—'

'Hush,' she whispered, touching his lips with soft fingers. 'Let's not talk about it. Talking about things always makes them seem more real, and this isn't real, Nik. It can't be. Love brings too much pain, Nik. Too much for me to ever love again.'

He reached up to grasp her wrist and tell her that was nonsense, but she'd moved before he could touch her, and only the pattern of light her torch showed in the corridor from time to time reminded him that she was sharing the lonely night vigil.

CHAPTER FIVE

ELLIE was cupping and tapping Patrick's back, encouraging him to cough, when an awareness, like a breeze across her skin, made her turn.

'Your friend Josie is awake and aware,' Nik said, his smile failing to mask the drawn lines of tiredness on his face.

'Seizures?' Ellie asked, hoping she sounded medically focused, though enough turbulence to qualify for the same name was happening inside her.

'Not as yet.'

The tired smile brightened, lit a spark in his dark eyes, and Ellie smiled back, sharing his triumph.

'Wouldn't it be great?' she said, not mentioning the hope they both shared that Josie might remain seizure-free, in case saying it reminded the fates to throw more bad luck the child's way.

'We won't know for some time. She'll need to be watched. I'm sending Jack in with Len to the clinic in town, and Jasmine can stay here to special Josie. I'll have a few hours' sleep then go in to town myself. I need to see the clinic operations.'

He held up his hand as Ellie began her protest.

'I'll take Carl, it's all organised. He's hoping to find some things he needs to get the gas tanks reconnected. Apparently some shops are still operating. He tells me there's plenty of gas in the tanks here on the mine site, and he wants to connect the tanks to the big ovens in the kitchen. Use gas—save electricity. He and Jack can come back, and Len and I will finish the clinic together.'

'Just as long as you do,' Ellie told him. 'It's easy to feel safe here in the camp, where we can't hear the sound of gunfire, but the situation's so unstable, Nik…'

She couldn't go on—couldn't put into words a sudden fear she had for him. And in that moment she knew, beyond doubt, that it was too late not to fall in love again.

She was there—fallen—because the stab of pain she'd felt at the *thought* of Nik being injured was but a precursor of what would follow if anything happened to him.

He must have heard something in her voice, or seen it in her eyes, for he hesitated. Then a cry from Josie's room made him turn away, but not before he'd breathed her name—just 'Ellie', but so softly and tenderly spoken she felt her insides liquefy and the tremble return to her knees.

'It's impossible,' she said to Patrick as she returned to trying to loosen the foreign matter in his lungs. 'Ridiculous! Why him? Why now? Honestly, Patrick, this is not the way things work. I could accept attraction, but love doesn't just hit you like a lightning strike, or that ridiculous image of a little cherub firing arrows. It can't work that way—it's too random, accidental—terrible matches could be made.'

She tapped, hand cupped, across his chest, while the little boy, head turned on the pillow, smiled, certain whatever she was saying was meant for him.

'Not that this will ever be a match. He's engaged, though he doesn't seem too sure about it, and I don't want to fall in love again. In lust maybe, an affair maybe, but love? No way, Patrick.'

Patrick coughed, then smiled again, and tentatively tried out a few of Ellie's phrases.

'Fall in love again?' he said.

'Never!' Ellie told him, though as she said it memories of the loneliness she'd felt these last eight years flooded her mind. Times she'd come home from work, as high as a kite because a child had been saved, or flatter than a lizard because one had been lost. And there'd been no one to share either the joy or the sorrow, no one with whom she'd been able to dance out her delight; no strong arms to hold her as she'd wept hot, angry, despairing tears into his shirt.

And suddenly she could see Nik in that role—holding her, sharing her pain.

Dancing with delight?

That was more difficult to visualise as he was such a self-contained man. Emotionless, she'd have said until the kiss...

'Ellie loves Patrick?'

Ellie looked down at the little boy and smiled.

'So much,' she said, and gave him a big, tight hug. 'Ellie loves you so much, and she loves Harry, and Josie, and all the other children in the camp.'

She knew he didn't understand her, but she felt better thinking about the children, about why she was here in Erireka, which was to help children like Patrick and Harry and Josie—not to fall in love.

'Definitely not fall in love,' she said, more to herself than to Patrick, but, of course, he picked it up, and Ellie shook her head, wondering just when he'd drop that gem into a conversation.

She just hoped it wouldn't be to Nik.

Nik woke from a short but deep sleep, refreshed yet uneasy, as if there was something he had to do—or something he'd failed to do before he'd slept. A mental scan didn't reveal the source of the trouble, although the number of times his scanner bumped into images of Ellie reminded him of the strange things that had happened between the two of them the previous day.

He decided to put his renewed feelings towards her down to a combination of tiredness from the journey and the stress he'd been under prior to undertaking it. It should be OK because he was pretty sure she'd been definite about not wanting to get involved with him, and he'd certainly told her he was engaged, so there was no reason why everything shouldn't go back to normal between them.

This bit of introspection seemed to banish the vague concern he'd had on waking, so he felt confident about tackling the day ahead.

The confidence lasted until he was walking across to the dining room to grab a snack before going into town and saw a tall, slim figure walking away from it in the other direction. *Sto Diablo!* Did the woman never obey orders?

Never get the sleep she needed to keep operating at an efficient level?

His angry reaction, born of concern for her, for the sleep deprivation she was suffering, was replaced by worry. She knew she had to sleep, so something must be wrong.

He followed her, his long strides eating up the ground between them.

She held something—a basin, not a tray—in her hands, her attention focused on not spilling whatever was in it. In which case he shouldn't startle her by calling to her.

He overtook her as she reached the furthest of the shipping containers.

'And just what do you think you're doing?'

Startled grey eyes swung towards him.

'Nik, I thought you'd have left by now. Oh, Nik!'

The desperate appeal in her voice as she spoke his name the second time wiped any last remnants of anger from his mind, replacing it with a desire to do anything he could to clear away the distress that was now written clearly on her features.

She hesitated, then straightened up, as if the unspoken plea in the way she'd said his name had been nothing more than momentary weakness.

'I can manage. She's not badly hurt—but she's just a child. Children playing soldiers— it's so wrong, but if it's all they've ever known...'

She broke off, shaking her head.

'I'll explain later. You go to town, do what you have to do.'

A pause, then she repeated, 'Later!'

He wanted to demand answers, tell her 'later' wasn't good enough, but she was so obviously upset he couldn't add to whatever burden she already carried. He touched her lightly on the shoulder and walked back the way he'd come, only realising as he reached the dining room the incongruity of what she'd been holding.

A bowl of water, clouded, no doubt by antiseptic of some kind, a string bag with cotton swabs and dressings and a camera.

A camera?

He had no time to puzzle over it. Carl was in the kitchen, chatting to Ben while he waited for Nik.

'I've managed to persuade Arwon to let us take the truck, which means we won't have to sit on the tray while the brat pack ride in the cabin.'

Nik nodded his appreciation, thanked Ben for a hearty sandwich he'd produced and suggested Carl drive while he ate.

'To save some time,' he added, though his mind wasn't on the trip to town. It was firmly fixed on an overheated shipping container, and whatever new injury Ellie was handling within it.

He found out that evening, when he discovered she'd assembled all the soldiers in the dining room after the evening meal. Using the basic Erirekan she knew, and Arwon as an interpreter for what she didn't know, she delivered an impassioned plea for an end to the war.

Nik had pieced some of this together from the English parts of her speech, but still wasn't prepared for the shock tactics at the end, though why she'd had the camera hanging from her shoulder now became clear.

'You don't realise how it's affecting all the people of the island—particularly the children. What if this was your child? Your little sister?' she cried in English, her Erirekan forgotten in her emotional plea.

She passed around Polaroid photos of a young girl who couldn't have been more than eleven. They'd obviously been taken before the bowl of water had been used to clean her up, so the bright red blood on her face and legs and the ugly black singeing of the burn to her arms were clearly visible.

'This happened in play!' Ellie told them. 'Children's play has always mimicked adult life—girls playing with dolls as babies, playing house, boys pretending to go hunting. But all these children see is fighting, and this girl was playing war. See the burns. From a "pretend" bomb one of the boys made, while the cuts are from barbed wire as she tried to escape her own burning clothes. Your war is reaching out to hurt the children, not only in the disruption of their daily lives but even in their play!'

Nik heard the passion in her words and understood it, for he, too, was haunted by the long-term psychological damage of war on children.

'This wasn't done deliberately?' he asked Ellie, when she finished speaking. 'You're sure it was in play?'

She nodded, as if all her energy had been expended, leaving none for words. Nik watched the soldiers pass the photos from hand to hand, some of them looking away, others shaking their heads, because they, too, were only children, playing war for real—risking death without fully understanding that it was for ever.

What could he—one man—do to make amends?

He couldn't stop a war he didn't understand, but he could be practical.

'Did you shift her to the hospital?'

Ellie had been watching the photos pass among the men, frowning at those who turned away so they were shamed into looking. Now she swung towards him, and he saw a little warmth creep back into her eyes and a tight smile form on her lips.

'No,' she said quietly, moving away from the men towards an open door. 'She's not as badly hurt as the photos make it look. The burns are superficial, the tears from the wire not deep. We'll have to be cautious about infection setting in, but she wanted to stay with her mother and family and that seemed the best option. Though they're living in a shipping container, it's as close to normality as she's likely to get right now.'

Once again he was aware of how closely their thoughts were attuned. Though he was even more aware of the attraction weaving between them like the threads of some invisible net. Maybe it hadn't been a build-up of stress and travel tiredness after all.

'They were playing outside the wire when it happened,' Ellie went on to explain. 'And her scream woke me—see, I *was* sleeping—but by the time I arrived her mother had carried her back inside. I've started her on a hefty dose of antibiotics to try to stop any infection...'

Ellie couldn't finish, too full of anguish for a world where 'play' could so easily have burnt a child to death to find words.

But Nik couldn't have needed them, for he stepped forward and grasped her shoulders, easing her out through the doorway before drawing her close, then wrapping his arms around her, giving the physical comfort that went far beyond speech—even beyond thought.

'We'll get her better,' he promised, his lips brushing against her ear the way a lover's might have.

Nik as lover was a dark and dangerous thought, and Ellie retreated from it, finding refuge in the young girl's plight.

'We'll get her better physically,' she told his shoulder, compelled to reveal her deepest fears. 'But mentally? Do these children ever get over the damage war brings in its wake?'

'I was wondering that myself. About long-term damage,' Nik admitted. 'And I have to believe they do—that children are resilient enough to put it behind them.' His tone made a promise of the words.

Yet still Ellie couldn't believe.

'Maybe if it's short term—the war, I mean. Maybe if it doesn't go on and on, so it becomes all they know and they grow up with the certain knowledge they'll be part of it eventually.'

'We've come to help civilians, Ellie, not to get involved politically—not to stop wars, even if we could.'

Nik said the words, murmuring them against the softness of her hair, but at the same time something deep within him was denying them. Something was suggesting that helping through medicine was no longer enough.

'We could try,' she said, straightening up and moving out of his arms. 'I know Rani. I could talk to him. Show him the photos—talk about the long-term effect of war on children. Tell him about children needing security and love. Surely there's an understanding of love, especially love for children, in the hearts of men on both sides of this stupid fight.'

'There must be,' Nik agreed, kissing her lightly on the cheek. 'Especially in a place like this, where the people have lived surrounded by such wonderful natural beauty. We're here, perched on the edge of an ugly hole in the ground, but look up at the stars—listen to the sounds of the ocean battering against the reef, hear the jungle breathing.'

He watched her scan the inky sky, and saw her smile at the brightness of the stars.

'Without love,' he said quietly, sharing a scrap of philosophy he'd found within himself in another fraught situation, 'this world would have self-destructed aeons ago. Melted in upon itself because of the barbarity of its people. There has to be more good than bad. Deep down, you know that. And where there's good, Ellie, there's also love.'

He drew her close again and Ellie felt her body relax against his strong one, while the words rang in her head like some paean of hope to the future. Then she realised two things. One, she'd never heard Nik speak like that before. Nik, the practical, turning poetic?

The second realisation was even more worrying. For someone trying not to be in love with the man who held her in his arms, she was behaving in an extremely stupid way by remaining there, although her body kept suggesting it had found the haven it had been seeking for a long, long time.

Danger as deep as quicksand in that thought! Yet when he kissed her, she didn't move away.

Instead, she tilted her head so she could kiss him back, pretending it was thanks for the comfort his words had given her, but when she moved her tongue against the shape of his lips, tested the hardness of teeth and entered the warm cavern of his mouth, she knew it wasn't thanks, but passion driving her.

Driving him, too, if the pressure of his hands as they explored her body was any guide.

Light years later, or only minutes, she pushed away.

'I must go—Jazzy's covering for me until I get to work.'

'Of course,' he said softly, but the look on his face denied his agreement. He wanted her to stay as much as she longed to remain in his arms. But he recovered first.

'The injured girl?' he asked.

'I'll check on her before I start at the hospital,' she assured him, looking into his dark eyes, wishing she could read his thoughts as easily as he apparently read hers. 'Her mother and the women who are tending her know to call me if there's any change at all. I think they were as shocked as I was by the extent of the injuries caused through children's ''play''.'

'I'm sure they were,' he said, and she knew from the sudden tiredness in his voice that, for all his words of faith in humankind, the episode had struck as deep into his heart as it had into hers.

Or was it something else that made him frown?

The second kiss?

The radar that operated between them failed her, for she couldn't answer her own question.

Nik watched her walk away, then went back inside and gathered up her photos, sliding them into his pocket without looking at them again— knowing the images were already imprinted on his mind.

Yet though his medical mind was on the psychological effects of war on children, the rest of him was humming with the memories of Ellie's body soft against his, leaning on his hardness, as if his strength alone could see her through her despair for the children of war.

Then, as his body had taken the closeness a different way, stirring to desire against all his better judgement and good taste, he'd kissed her, and when she'd kissed him back he'd known she was the woman he wanted to hold in his arms for ever.

She and no other—what did the marriage lines say? Forsaking all others? Hell, he'd do that in a flash.

But forsaking Lena, the daughter of his father's best friend—the woman chosen for him by two determined and autocratic men—would mean forsaking much else beside.

Forsaking KidCare!

His muttered curses this time were in Greek, a language he found far more expressive for his frustration.

He didn't want the fortune or the half-share in the shipping company, which his father had made conditional on his marriage to Lena, but without the income from it he couldn't continue to fund either the clinics he'd set up in poor areas of cities around the world, neither could he continue to take teams like this into war- or famine-ravaged areas.

He made his way back to the house, feeling the cool night air soothe his heated skin, looking up again at the myriad stars. This beautiful place—this paradise—made ugly first by commerce, then by greed and war. Yet commerce paid for what he did, what hope he offered children, so who was he to deny it?

He shrugged away the thoughts and forced himself to think not of war, or Ellie, but of work.

He had notes on the way the town clinic was running, ideas that he wanted to think through, and Jack was doing a stocktake of the drugs and dressings the first members of the team had brought with them, so they could keep track of what they had or what would need to be ordered before the next flight. It didn't matter where you went in the world, paperwork followed.

Ellie spent a lot of the night with Josie. Though Nik had pronounced her out of danger, concern she might have seizures remained.

And sitting by the child's bed, her thoughts, though tempted to think of Nik, turned resolutely to the injured child—and to all the children of the island.

Did she feel so strongly about their fate because she'd lost her own child? Was this why she felt compelled to do something? Or had the block of ice in which she'd frozen her heart when Dave and Aaron had died begun to melt, so her concern was going deeper—becoming more personal?

'The clinic doesn't open on weekends,' she announced to Nik, when he walked into the hospital soon after dawn. She was so full of the plans she'd worked on during the night she didn't bother with greeting him, and talking seemed a good way of covering up the hitch of excitement her body had felt when he'd appeared.

'That means Len and Jazzy will be here to cover the hospital work. I thought I'd go up into the hills and see Rani. Take the photos. I know he deserted us, but before that, while he was teaching us the language, he and I got on well. He has a wife—it's why he wanted to come back, because she's pregnant. I know you'll say it won't do any good, but I have to try, Nik. I have to speak to his men, too. To try to stop this war before it becomes such an accepted way of life nothing will stop it.'

The words rushed out, stumbling over each other in their haste to put her case across. She knew he'd argue, but if she kept talking, maybe she could sway him.

'Impossible! Ridiculous!'

OK, so he wasn't swayed so far.

'You know you can't do that. How would you find their camp, for a start? Do you think there'll be signposts? And if there were, wouldn't Arwon's lot have followed them by now? You need more sleep, obviously, because in a normal, rested state you would have realised just how utterly absurd your idea is.'

Disapproval was emanating from him so strongly Ellie was sure she could see it spark in the air between them. It blazed in his eyes, and bleached his lips to whiteness.

'I've got to try,' she said, using memories of the child's injuries—from *play* of all things—to fire anger, needing to match her heat to his before he burnt away her resolution. 'I'm bloody going!'

'I forbid it,' he growled, his voice so cold it was like a sliver of ice sliding down her spine.

'The weekend is my time off. You can't forbid it because you can't control what I do with my own time.'

'I *can* forbid it because you're a member of my team and I'm responsible for your safety. What kind of a leader would I be if I let you put your stupid head into such an obvious noose? You could be taken hostage—you wouldn't even have to be kidnapped, because you'd walked in by yourself, to be taken prisoner by them, held to ransom—then what happens? *I'm* supposed to bail you out?'

'Of course not,' Ellie said, with what dignity she could muster, though what seemed like an over-reaction on Nik's part had shaken her. 'Once they realise I'm not worth anything to anyone, they'd soon let me go.'

'Not worth anything to anyone? Not *worth* anything to anyone?'

Apparently the argument became too much for him at this stage, so he stormed out of the hospital, waving his arms in the air, which, had it been Greek air, would have been turning blue.

Ellie finished her morning duties, helped Paul with breakfasts, then walked across to the container where the injured girl lived.

Nik had every right to be angry with her. What she intended doing was stupid, and irresponsible, but the only life she'd be endangering would be her own, and since the accident which had snatched her husband and infant son from her eight years ago, she hadn't put a lot of value on it.

Not that she didn't enjoy living—she did. She also knew she had plenty to give to others in a practical sense and had tried to do that, both in her everyday work and in volunteering. But if the rebels decided to keep her, or even kill her, who would suffer? A few friends? A cousin she was close to?

As she walked into the hot, dark space, she acknowledged these were thoughts she'd often had when she'd been in dangerous situations, but this time they didn't carry the conviction that had always calmed her and allowed her to direct all her energies to what had to be done.

But when she knelt beside the child and saw, in the dim light shed by a kerosene lamp, the pain in the huge, dark eyes, she knew she'd have to go through with her plan whether Nik liked it or not.

Whether this new inner self liked it or not...

Exhaustion must have caught up with her, for she slept all day. In her own bed, as Millie, now diagnosed as having chickenpox, had been shifted to the hospital. Waking too late to help Paul with the dinners, she approached the hospital cautiously. Nik hadn't been in the dining room when she'd grabbed a meal, neither had she seen him at the house. But her caution wasn't warranted—he wasn't at the hospital either.

'Nik?' Paul echoed, when she had to ask. 'Last I saw of him he was over by the containers. Carl found an old blowtorch and they were cutting holes in the sides to make windows. They're going to rig up sheets of plastic that can be lowered over these openings in case of rain.'

Ellie frowned—why hadn't she thought of cutting holes to provide more ventilation?—then had to smile at her irrational irritation. Though their minds were so often in tune, Nik was practical in ways she could never be, while her thought processes were better suited to people than to things.

Still, whatever he was doing—cutting holes, although it was getting dark—as long as it was away from where she was, that was fine with her. She had a lot to think about and certainly didn't need Nik's presence short-circuiting her mind or confusing her body.

Though before Paul went off duty, she should duck across to furthest of the containers to check on the young girl.

And had Nik seen the pregnant woman to-day?

Ellie followed Paul into the boys' room, where he was collecting the plates from their evening meal.

'The emaciated pregnant woman?' he said, in reply to her question. 'Yes, Maze brought her to the clinic. According to Maze, she's eating and drinking, which I think's a good sign she might accept this baby.'

'I hope so,' Ellie said, her heart cramping at the thought the newborn might be abandoned, though understanding why the woman could choose to take that course.

'And your young girl,' Paul continued. 'The one the women are nursing. Nik sent Jasmine to see her when Jazzy got back from town and there's no sign of infection so far.'

Ellie thought she was thankful, but she was still so confused over her feelings for Nik, and mentally distressed over the 'play' incident, she couldn't pin down a 'thankful' in the morass of her thoughts.

She said goodnight to Paul and checked on all her patients. One of the chickenpox victims had been discharged, so there was a spare bed in the end room and another in the old man's room.

Josie was awake and alert, chatting to her mother, who was sitting on the edge of Millie's bed, sponging the sick woman's skin with cool water. The scene made Ellie smile. At first the local people had acted as if the hospital frightened them—almost as if they thought it a place of death. They would bring their loved ones, but leave them and not visit, not even sit with them for a few minutes. But things were changing. Harry's father was in with him, tapping Harry's chest in the way Paul must have shown him. Now Josie's mother had returned—*and* was helping out.

'Paul says this is new—the families visiting.'

Ellie jerked with surprise, then spun to face the man who'd spoken. Not cutting holes in containers at all.

'It is,' she agreed, hoping the manifestations of delight her traitorous body was experiencing weren't visible on her skin. Then she smiled because she had to, for many reasons, but especially because the visits were a sign the local people were accepting them. 'It's great, isn't it?'

If she thought he was going to smile back, she was in for a disappointment, Nik thought, glowering at the woman whose smile had made her skin glow. He'd spent the entire day finding things to do so he didn't have to think about her, or the insane idea she was carrying in her head, now here she was, smiling and glowing, as if she hadn't a care in the world and wasn't the cause of his rumbling volcano of mental torment.

'I saw the pregnant woman and sent Jazzy to see your young girl,' he said, feeling bad now because both her smile and the glow had faded.

'Yes, Paul told me. Thank you,' she said formally, then she added, 'If there's nothing else?' in a polite 'nurse' voice, hesitated a moment and walked away.

He should go after her and throttle her. It would save her from whatever fate the rebels in the hills might have in store for her—because he had no doubt she intended to go through with her rash plan—and, better still, it would release a lot of *his* tension.

Instead, he returned to the main house, hoping to find one of the soldier boys who hung around there and send him to find Arwon. He seemed to understand English so perhaps Nik could gather some ammunition from him—of the verbal kind—to add to the next argument he would inevitably have with Ellie.

'The hill people should have supported us, not fought us,' Arwon told him, when Nik had made coffee for them both and they'd settled into comfortable lounge chairs abandoned—and, no doubt, regretted—by the mine manager's wife when she'd been told to leave.

'They didn't?' Nik prompted.

'At first they did, but then they took the opportunity to settle old scores with the lowlanders.'

Arwon spat the last word out, surprising Nik enough for him to ask, 'You're not a lowlander yourself?'

'I'm a soldier,' Arwon told him. 'I have no allegiance except to my country of Erireka. More people should remember it is the whole country which is suffering from this strife, not just one tribe or another.'

Nik thought back to what he knew of the original attacks on the mine.

'Were the soldiers acting for the whole country when they overthrew the government then co-ordinated the attacks on the mine and sent the mining company personnel packing?'

A dangerous question but he had to work out where things stood if the team was to do any long-term good. And lingering in the back of his mind was the suspicion that maybe he *did* have a responsibility to do more than patch the wounds of war. Maybe Ellie was right in wanting to take positive action, though she was certainly wrong—impossibly wrong—in the way she intended going about it.

Putting all thoughts of Ellie firmly out of his head, he tuned back in to what Arwon was telling him.

'The government had weakened. They watered down the demands they had promised to make on the company and failed to get a proper share of the profits from the minerals the company took from our soil.'

Nik knew this was an argument used in many places, but, from what he'd read and learned before coming to Erireka, in this case the company here had been fair.

'What did you consider was a proper share?' he asked Arwon.

'Half!'

The reply was so swift, Nik knew it must have been a huge bone of contention, but now he was even more puzzled.

'Weren't you getting half? I'm sorry, I don't know a lot about it, but I thought I'd read that the proceeds were split fifty-fifty.'

'They were supposed to be.' Arwon's dark skin was flushed with anger. 'But the company cheated. They paid us fifty per cent after tax— after they had written off costs and capital expenditure and so much else, our country ended up with a pittance.'

Nik's astonishment must have shown in his face, for Arwon nodded and said, 'Check the figures for yourself. It's true!'

'I believe you,' Nik assured him. 'I just can't believe all of Erireka isn't behind you in this. I would have thought such injustice would have united the people, not brought about civil war.'

'It did at first,' Arwon admitted. 'Then we saw how badly things were going for the people with the mine gone, and we wanted to negotiate with the company again. Rani and his lot said, no, we should run the mine ourselves, and when that didn't work, the hill people blamed the low-landers who had worked here, but they had worked under orders—not as managers and geologists.'

'What a stupid mess!' Nik muttered, then realised, as his companion stiffened, it hadn't been the wisest of remarks.

'Don't worry, Arwon, I'm not saying you're stupid, I'm just frustrated by how easily things can get out of hand. Have you tried to talk peace with Rani and his men?'

'Not with Rani. Never with Rani! We sent him from the island for the trouble he caused, and when he sneaked back he made sure I didn't see him. He hid on the plane—in the cockpit where we don't go to unload—then ran away in the dark, the mongrel cur.'

'But *could* you talk to him?' Nik persisted, cutting through the emotion to get at where things stood now.

'He would have to come to me,' Arwon said, then, with a certain relish in his voice, he added, 'And he won't do that. Lose too much face with his men—lose his place as leader—and then what good would talking to him do?'

Nik had no reply, and though they talked for a while longer, he didn't learn anything more.

Arwon's obvious dislike of Rani made Nik hold back from mentioning Ellie's plan. There were always wheels within wheels in these situations, and he wouldn't put it past Arwon's lot capturing Ellie themselves, if only to throw the blame on the rebels.

So, though the conversation had opened his eyes to what had started the conflict, it hadn't helped with regard to Ellie's dangerous idea. Anger hadn't worked, and in hindsight he regretted his outburst. Far better to have spoken calmly and rationally to her, but the thought of her putting herself into such danger, then saying no one would care what happened to her—well, no man would have been able to control his temper in the face of such provocation!

Knowing her well enough to be sure she intended going ahead with it, he also knew he'd have to think of some way to dissuade her.

Locking her up in an unused shipping container was all he could be certain would work, and his mind drifted off, playing with an image that had sneaked under his guard—he and Ellie both locked up together, just the two of them. The first thing he'd do would be to kiss her again, because he was almost certain kisses couldn't taste the way his memory of that kiss suggested.

Then, after a long, long time, when he'd done kissing her lips, he'd kiss her skin, just near her ear, and her temple, and her eyelids—feel her silky skin beneath his lips…

His body stirred, shaming him from his imaginings.

He had to stop Ellie going into the hills if it was the last thing he did. And as far as any relationship with her was concerned—or any future friendship—it probably *would* be the last thing he did!

Not that he could have a relationship with her—not and keep KidCare going.

He found himself swearing again, then realised it was becoming a habit. He'd inherited his father's gold worry beads. Maybe he should start using them.

CHAPTER SIX

SHE was avoiding him. Nik knew it, but didn't go out of his way to seek Ellie out. How he felt when he caught glimpses of her—striding between the hospital and the kitchen early in the morning, then later, from the hospital to the house—was enough to remind him that not seeing her was a good thing.

Nik kept busy, checking the hospital patients first, then leaving them with Paul and a new local helper, so he could finish working on the windows he and Carl were cutting in the shipping containers.

At midday he had to excuse himself from this task to take the afternoon clinic under the poinciana tree. Paul arrived to assist.

'I've left the hospital patients under Lurie's watchful eye. She'll call me if there's any problem—apart from patient complaints about the way she makes them lie tidily in bed. She'd have made a first-class matron in the old days when all the beds had to be made just so.'

'Has she been with you long? Today's the first day I've seen her.'

Paul looked worried, as if the simple question posed a dilemma for him.

'She's been here in camp for a long time,' he said. 'Ellie ferreted her out soon after we arrived and tried to persuade her to work for us because she's a trained nurse—did her training in Port Moresby. Ellie offered her paid work, like the helpers at the kitchen.'

'And she refused?'

'She said she was frightened. Apparently she'd been the nurse here at the mine, running a kind of first-aid station, and when the revolt against the mine took place, locals who'd worked here were targeted. Her home was burnt down and she felt it was a warning. Naturally, she didn't want to put herself into a similar situation, working with us.'

Nik sighed. It was the wheels-within-wheels situation again—and the ramifications of a war that wasn't going anywhere. Though some mystery remained.

'So why's she changed her mind now?'

'You! You'll be pleased to know you're now her god. Young Josie is her niece—you cured her and now you have a friend for life. In fact, knowing the intricate family relationships in most of these places, you've probably got a couple of dozen friends for life, out of that one op.'

'Well, I hope Josie doesn't go and die on us and they all turn into enemies for life,' Nik muttered, signalling to Paul to bring the first patient.

'I wondered if you could do a half-day at the town clinic tomorrow,' Len suggested, seeking Nik out much later in the day when he and Jasmine returned from town.

Nik had just seen the last of the clinic patients—a five-hour session without a break, though Paul had brought him watery coffee and a biscuit at some stage.

'Something specific?' Nik asked Len.

'Not really, just our patient numbers are up and there are a few people who came in today who need more diagnostic skills than either Jazzy or I have. I suggested they come back tomorrow.'

'Morning or afternoon?' Nik was thinking that if he wasn't there to do the afternoon clinic, then Ellie, though supposedly sleeping through the day, would find out by osmosis and insist on doing it.

'Doesn't matter. They'll come first thing and sit there until they see someone. I think word got around there was a doctor on the island—that would explain the increase in patient numbers.'

'I'll come in the morning. The three of us can go and I'll arrange for one of Arwon's boys to bring me back to camp for the afternoon clinic here.'

Len frowned at him.

'Ellie won't like that. She made a rule we only travel in pairs.'

Ellie would have to lump it, Nik thought, certain he'd established enough rapport with Arwon for him to trust the man to arrange secure transport.

And who was she to talk anyway, pursuing this insane idea of heading for the hills?

He knew he had to talk to her—to persuade her of the folly of this behaviour—but seeing her, he also knew, would stir up the new and tormentingly exciting feelings he had for her. They were bad enough when he didn't see her.

He was still in this state of indecision—which made checking stock with Jack after dinner very difficult—when the lad arrived. Chest heaving as he tried to regain his breath, he hurled a lot of incomprehensible words at the two men.

'Get Ellie from the hospital—she'll understand enough,' Nik said to Jack, while he, seeing blood staining the boy's ragged shorts, sat him down and began to examine him.

The boy pushed his hands away and pointed to the door, urgency in every gesture—fear, or something like it, in the tense muscles of his body.

Ellie arrived, also slightly breathless, which, to Nik's annoyance, drew his attention to her high, firm breasts. Oblivious to his reaction, she shot some questions at the boy, listened as he rattled off his problem, then turned to Nik.

'The truck's overturned on the road from the airstrip. I think, from what I can make out, on a tight bend where it comes around the mountain.'

'What transport do we have?'

'The car Len and Jazzy have been using. The boy doesn't know how many soldiers are trapped in the cabin, but there are rarely fewer than six travelling in that thing. We should take Len because he understands the car, Paul can take my place at the hospital and we can let Jazzy sleep until we bring in the injured, when we'll probably need everyone on hand.'

'I'll get Len, and send Paul over to the hospital,' Jack offered, speaking before Nik had time to remind Ellie that he was the boss of this outfit and should be making these decisions.

Though she had the experience to know how to deploy what staff they had, and he couldn't find any objection with her arrangements, except...

'Sounds good,' he said mildly, 'but you stay at the hospital and let Paul come with me and Len.'

He might have known she'd argue, and felt his brows draw together as she said, 'I'm fresher—less likely to make mistakes. Besides, I speak and understand far more Erirekan than Paul does. I'll grab some torches and lamps and an emergency first-aid kit. Perhaps a couple. Will you get the fluids? And we don't have jaws of life, but maybe tools like crowbars—and metal cutters. We'll need Carl, too.'

Nik stopped arguing, and nodded his agreement to finding some bags of fluid. And though he told himself there couldn't be any danger attached to her attending an accident scene in the company of several men, he was still worried for her, and angry with himself that it should be that way. This was the perfect example of why he'd wanted to put a 'no fraternisation' rule into place. Relationships between team members could be distracting, though, he admitted ruefully to himself, no rule in the world could prevent him being distracted, usually at inconvenient times, by thoughts of Ellie.

* * *

The battered old truck had come to rest against a boulder which stuck out from the mountain-side like a miniature, and very misplaced, lean-ing tower of Pisa. The good thing was that the truck had obviously rolled over as it had left the road, flattening the vines, ferns and small palms that grew in such abundance on the mountain slope, thus making access for the rescuers much easier.

Rolling over was also the bad thing, Ellie realised when they'd picked their cautious way down the steep slope. The sides of the cabin had been sufficiently damaged for the doors to be impossible to open, and though the windows and windscreen had all been shattered, the front of the cabin was hard up against the rock, and egress through the windscreen almost impossi-ble.

Carl, Len and Nik tested the security of the wreck first, eventually pronouncing themselves satisfied the boulder wasn't going to move and they could work on the vehicle without danger. Carl began rigging lights, and Ellie, with her torch, climbed up on the bonnet, hoping to see into the cabin and begin to assess the human cost.

'Get down off there—we can get more access from the rear window.' Nik was giving orders now, but Ellie had seen a hand reaching out through a small gap between the rock and the wreck, fingers waggling.

'There's at least one alive,' she said, adding a quiet 'at the moment' under her breath.

She grabbed the fingers and squeezed them, offering what little encouragement she could in her basic Erirekan. From the fingers she found the wrist, and was comforted to feel a strong pulse.

'Pulse strong,' she reported, although this wasn't all good. The boy—for it was a small hand—might be bleeding from a wound, and the strong pumping of his heart would hasten his death if they couldn't get him out.

She asked him where he was, but he either didn't hear or didn't understand her. Or perhaps he couldn't speak. She shone the torch through the opening, hoping to be able to see where the arm led, but, though she could see a press of flesh and clothing, it was impossible to distinguish one person from another.

So she held the hand and kept talking, using her free hand to feel around inside, hoping by touch to work out how many of the young soldiers were in the vehicle—feeling for dreadlocks in case Arwon had been with them.

A cold shiver played down her spine. Without Arwon, would the troubles escalate?

She could hear the rasp of metal and the screech of its protests, and told the boy whose hand she held not to worry—men were opening up the truck to get them out. Soon they'd be free.

Soon? It seemed hours before the opening around the rear window was wide enough for Nik to tell the men to stop.

'I'll need you here,' he said to Ellie.

She told the boy she'd be back and, after an extra squeeze, released her grip on his hand.

'Feel for a carotid pulse,' Nik told Len. 'If there's no pulse, we don't need to worry about doing more harm than good. If we can move even one of them, we'll be able to do more for the rest.'

'No pulse here,' Len eventually reported, and they concentrated on retrieving that first, but sadly lifeless, body. Doubly sad, Ellie realised when she saw it was the cheerful young lad who always wore a dirty but still colourful sarong around his lower body, instead of the camouflage trousers the others favoured.

They laid him respectfully on the ground beside the truck, then Nik took the lead, using his longer arms to feel among the others, squashed into an impossibly small space.

'I've got a faint pulse on the next fellow,' Nik announced. 'Your hands are smaller, Ellie. See if you can get a brace around his neck. Can you feel his head?'

The light failed to penetrate the darkness in the cabin and Nik's hands guided hers to the patient. She slid her hands over crinkly hair— not dreadlocks—a forehead, nose and down the cheek to chin and neck.

She and Nik were so close she wasn't sure which skin was hers, which his, but together they managed to secure the brace, then Nik guided her hands to the man's armpit on one side.

'If you can grasp him there, I'll take the other side. I know he may be jammed, or haemorrhage badly if we move him and release pressure on some wound, but even if we wait till dawn we might not be able to see much better.'

'And they might all be dead,' Ellie finished, getting herself into position so she could take her share of the man's weight.

She could hear Len and Carl working on cutting through the lower side of the vehicle, hoping to get better access that way, and reminded

herself the young soldiers were all slight—
barely more than boys.

'OK, lift,' Nik said, and slowly they tried to
draw the body they held between them upward.

The lad groaned, the movement stopped, then
he jerked, and though Ellie feared at first he
might have died, he must have been helping
them, perhaps kicking free of someone who'd
lain across his legs, for the lifting became easier
and soon they had a living, breathing young soldier out from the wreckage.

Was it the boy whose hand she'd held?

As she passed him to Carl and Len, she
looked at his hands and didn't think so.

Could they, by some miracle, save two young
lives from this mess?

'Take a look at him, Len, and call me if you
need me. Ellie, you talk to those still trapped,
see if you can get someone to answer you,' Nik
said, then he set a small torch between his teeth
and leaned into the now expanded space in the
cabin.

Ellie was shining her own torch into the
cabin, as she spoke quietly in the soft, sibilant
language. No one answered her, and all she
could see, apart from Nik's back, was a dark
tangle of limbs, shiny with sweat or blood, and
the duller sheen of hair or clothing.

'Another one with no pulse—if we get him out, we'll free the last one. I think there are only two in here now,' Nik reported, withdrawing and taking his torch from his mouth so he could speak. 'Carl, could you come up here? He's a big fellow, the next one.'

'Arwon?' Ellie asked, fearful again about their future if the leader was dead.

'I don't think so, though it's hard to tell,' Nik said, while she made way for Carl to take her place.

She slid off the tray and joined Len beside the patient they'd pulled out.

'How's he doing?'

'Fantastic, considering what he's been through. Left leg broken low down—could be tib and fib, I'm not sure. I'm making rough splints so we don't do more damage when we move him.'

Elle shuddered, wondering what damage they'd already done by hauling him out, marvelling at his courage to have kicked himself free as he had done.

'I think that big chap may have saved his mate's life,' Nik was saying to Carl, and she turned to see him bent over another young man, held securely on the sloping truck tray by Carl while Nik applied a pressure pad and bandages to a shoulder or upper arm wound.

'I thought you said the next one was already dead,' she said, as a nameless anxiety nagged at her senses.

'We moved him and felt blood spurt—realised we had to get this one out first. The dead man had fallen on this fellow—apparently in such a way he stopped the haemorrhage. I know it sounds callous, but I think we could safely leave the dead man in there until morning. We still have the problem of getting the wounded back to camp, and this guy needs urgent surgery so it's got to be stat.'

'But you said the dead man was a big fellow—there's someone else in there,' Ellie protested.

'I don't see how there could be,' Nik told her. 'You should see the size of the fellow we just moved. It's because of his size he's probably best left until morning. No one else could possibly have fitted in the cabin.'

Ellie wanted to argue she'd seen six or eight young soldiers squeeze into a cabin, but what was the point? She lifted the hand of the patient she'd been helping Len tend and squeezed the fingers, certain the size and shape were unfamiliar.

Len was fashioning stretchers to carry the wounded men to the car, while Nik was attaching a drip to the man with the injured artery. She checked her patient's pulse—strong and steady—and deserted him, taking the torch and climbing back up on the crushed bonnet.

No small, black fingers waving at her! Maybe she'd been wrong about the feel of them, yet her heart stuttered with anxiety and instinct told her she'd been right.

She shone her torch into the cabin, but when she tried to look inside, her head blocked out the torchlight. Nik was now off the tray, helping carry his patient up the slope, so he couldn't light up the interior for her.

She lay full length and felt around where she knew the child had been. Her fingers met skin, warm, with solid flesh beneath it. The dead man?

By touch she established it was him—huge, far bigger than anyone she'd met among the soldiers who frequented the camp. Carl and Nik had shifted him. Had they dropped him on the boy with the small hand?

She leaned further in and felt the truck move, as if she'd spoilt its precarious balance. But the balance wasn't precarious, she reminded herself. The men had checked that first.

She found a small shoulder, and was sure she felt it respond to her touch. Speaking gently, she used her sense of touch to work out where he was and why they hadn't reached him from the other side, then heard Nik calling to her. If she sat on someone's knee, they could all fit in the car to go back to the camp. Come along! What was she doing?

'There's someone else—a small person— trapped down in the footwell on the driver's side. The steering-wheel has caged him, and the body's fallen across that.'

'I have to take the haemorrhaging fellow back to camp. You come up and I'll send Len down. Carl can bring the car back and they'll get him out.'

'No, you all go. I'll stay with him, he knows me,' Ellie called back, and though she had no doubt Nik was muttering about bloody obstinate women, she guessed the situation with his patient was too dangerous for him to waste time arguing.

She stayed lying across the bonnet, stroking the boy's skin, talking quietly, praying he wasn't dead but not knowing, because she couldn't find his wrist or chin, just a bit of what she thought was his back and shoulder.

Although she doubted it was more than fifteen minutes, it seemed like hours before Carl returned, and longer still for him to fashion a kind of sling under the dead man's armpits. This he attached to a rope which he passed over the overhanging branch of a tree and, pulling together, they managed to drag the dead man free.

'You get the boy,' Carl told her, as he struggled to free the body from the rope. 'Nik wanted us straight back. We've already wasted time.'

While Carl set the dead man on the ground beside his compatriot, Ellie clambered up onto the tray and squeezed into the cabin. The boy—he was too small to be anything else—was where she'd imagined him, but now that she could shine her torch around, she could also see how she might be able to get him out. Carl had a crowbar, and if they could lever the steering-wheel out of the way, the child could slide free.

He was conscious—brown eyes, so wide open there was a rim of white around the iris, staring fixedly at her in the torchlight. In shock, by the look of him. But why wouldn't he be? She kept talking to him while she felt about his body, searching for obvious damage. He returned the pressure she applied to both hands, and when she tickled the soles of his feet, he drew them away. A good indication there was no spinal damage.

Explaining she'd be back, she clambered out, then gave Carl the torch so he could see the situation for himself.

She could hear him banging things and cursing softly to himself, but finally he withdrew and turned towards her.

'I'll take you back to camp and bring Ben back with me. I don't think we can shift the steering column, but we could cut through from the other side. It'll take time and time's what you don't have. Nik wants you in Theatre with him. He told me to get you back A.S.A.P.'

'But that means leaving boy here on his own.'

'We'll have to.' Carl was adamant. 'It won't be for long. The kid seems OK—scared but OK. That other fellow—the one Nik's operating on—he needs help bad.'

Ellie wanted to point out that with Len, Paul and Jazzy in camp, and only one nurse needed at the hospital, Nik would already have two helpers, but before she could put her protest into words she had to admit it was tight. One nurse had to be at the hospital, one would be needed to monitor the patient—a stand-in anaesthetist—which would only leave one person to assist, pass instruments and clear debris.

With the less-than-miraculous anaesthetics they had available, preparing the man for the operation would have taken a while, then cleaning the wound before repairs could begin a little longer. Nik shouldn't be too far advanced with it.

Excuses—that was all they were. She was needed at the house but didn't want to leave the child, trapped in the wreckage, frightened and alone. Reluctantly, she turned towards the boy, haltingly explaining she had to go for more help to get him out, and that she'd be back very soon.

It was a lie, the bit about her returning, and she knew she should never lie to children, but neither time nor her Erirekan extended to explaining the circumstances. Soon Carl and Ben would come back and free him. With luck he'd be on his own for no more than twenty minutes. But she still felt terrible as she accompanied Carl back to the car, and regret nagged at her.

Arriving at the main house, she made her way to the storeroom, where Jack's tidy housekeeping meant she had no trouble finding a scrub suit. As she entered the makeshift theatre, Nik looked up from what he was doing, nodding acknowledgement of her presence, though she guessed he wasn't pleased with her.

'Glad you could join us, Nurse Reardon,' he said smoothly. 'Done chasing ghosts?'

'It wasn't a ghost—it was a child,' Ellie shot right back at him. 'He's trapped in the cabin of the truck and we've left him all alone. It's dark and he's terrified.'

'Meanwhile, this man's bleeding to death. Ellie, you know about priorities. Scrub and put on gloves then come and hold this clamp. Len's doing what he can, but he hasn't got four hands.'

Ellie hurried to obey, guilt that she hadn't been here to help earlier vying with the remorse which had been churning inside her since leaving the young boy.

Pressing in between Nik and Len, she took the clamp Nik was holding with his left hand while teasing tissue from the torn artery with a scalpel held in his right. Ellie held the clamp, which cut off the flow of blood from the heart, while Len mopped at the blood which had already spread through the wound, finally revealing the vessel, torn when the man's shoulder must have struck something sharp with great force.

'Subclavian?' she guessed, and Nik nodded.

'Below where it branches to the ear, brain and spinal cord, but right now his left arm isn't getting much blood.'

With infinite patience Nik teased away at something Ellie couldn't see, but she felt his relief when the body pressed against her relaxed.

'Jackpot!' he said, holding up a small bloody scrap of bone. 'Whatever he hit broke his clavicle, and with such force the bone shattered. The jagged end must have torn the artery. I thought I had it fixed but when I tried to match up the ends of the clavicle, they didn't meet, so there had to be a bit of bone missing.'

He sounded so pleased this must be good news, but Ellie didn't understand.

'And that's it?' she said, as he dropped the piece into a dish on the tray and bent over his patient once again. 'But wouldn't the clavicle have mended if you put the two ends you had back together? I mean, you can hardly stick a loose bit of bone in there anyway.'

He moved slightly away from her, still working on the torn artery, telling her when to release the clamp for a few seconds then retighten it.

'I didn't need the piece to complete the jigsaw puzzle,' he explained, his tone softer now, as if finding the piece of bone had eased his tension. He was inserting tiny stitches in the walls of the torn vessel as he spoke. 'I needed to make sure it wasn't in the artery. Imagine how we'd all feel if we put this bloke back together then he had a heart attack because we'd left a chunk of bone blocking his artery.'

Duh! How stupid can you be?

Ellie silently berated herself for her stupidity, but concern for the boy was blurring her thought processes. She hoped it was concern for the boy, not physical proximity to Nik.

And why now, this feeling that went beyond physical attraction to Nik, when she'd known him, on and off, for years? She'd admired him, too, because he got things done. He was more emotional than she was—roaring when things went wrong, ripping into workers who weren't doing their jobs—but a pussy cat where kids were concerned, and a gentle, caring, careful, tactful doctor to patients of whatever sex, race, creed or colour.

'OK, release it completely and let's see how we've done.' Nik's instruction reminded her she should be concentrating on the man's actions, not the man himself. She released the clamp and felt the sudden tension in the air as they all held their breath while they waited to see if the stitches held.

'Yahoo! Yippee! You got it!' Paul expressed the delight of all of them, and though everyone was pleased Nik's next words brought them back to reality.

'We've still got to patch up the shoulder and then worry about infection. I'll leave a drain in place. We'll need to watch him carefully. In the hospital would be easier from a staffing point of view, but I can't risk him picking up chickenpox when his health's already compromised.'

'Put him in a room here,' Ellie suggested. 'We can set up the living room as another ward. We can move my bed in there. Jazzy and I can share a bed—we never sleep at the same time. Maybe the broken leg should go in there as well.'

'And nurse him how?'

She knew Nik felt the nursing resources were already stretched too thin, but she knew they would manage somehow.

'We'll sort that out!' she told him. 'It's what nurses do. Doctors might be gods in situations like this, picking bits of bone out of torn arteries, but nurses are the ones who adapt to developing situations, who make do, take on extra workloads and see the patient through in the end.'

Nik heard the defiance in her voice. She was as angry with him as he'd been with her earlier, when she'd refused to leave the crash site and he'd had been in torment over leaving her alone in the darkness. He'd already been upset over her rash idea to visit Rani before they'd left for the scene of the accident, and his concern for her had shifted to anger. Then, working with her body pressed against his had distracted him in ways he'd never experienced on the job before. He was more annoyed with himself than he was with her, but he couldn't help feeling she was the cause of both his rage and his distraction.

He bit back on both, as a solution to at least one of his problems struck him.

'Well, I'm glad we can rely on nurses,' he said, keeping his voice deliberately neutral, 'because it'll be a week at least before this chap is out of the woods, and the other soldier will need careful watching as well. In this climate, by the time I get to fixing his leg, infection could already have set in.'

He smiled to himself behind the mask. No way, after her declaration of nurses' dedication, could she take herself off on a wild-goose chase in the hills next weekend.

A stiffening in her body told him she'd got the message, but she didn't reply, contenting

herself with a slight jab of one elbow into his
rib cage as she shifted position beside him.

Then, as she muttered, so only he could hear,
'I'll go next weekend,' he realised she'd probably just been counting to ten before she'd spoken—cooling the hot temper he knew she hid
behind her air of quiet dignity.

And while it was that quiet dignity that had
first attracted him—years back—it had been
watching her explode that had heightened the
attraction—the idea that this reserved woman
had such fire hidden deep within her had, even
then, been infinitely exciting…

Skase! His body was stirring again. He had to
stop remembering—steel himself against the attraction torturing him with physical need.
Distraction was never good, but not being one
hundred per cent focused in a place like Erireka,
with serious problems waiting to erupt, could
make the difference between living and dying.

She moved to snip the thread he'd been using
to stitch the muscle, and the long length of her
body brushed against his, inadvertently this time
but still reminding him that wanting to resist attraction and actually resisting it were actions as
widely separated as the north and south poles.

CHAPTER SEVEN

IT WAS another hour before Nik was satisfied he'd done all he could for his patient. The still-comatose man was shifted into the living room, where Ellie, freed from the theatre earlier, had made up a bed for him and set up a barstool she'd nabbed from the dining room to act as a drip stand.

'Right,' she said to Paul, when with his and Len's help they'd settled the man into bed. 'It's close to midnight, so we'll go onto shorter shifts. You stay here.'

Nik, watching from the doorway, where he'd come to ask Ellie for help with the broken leg, stood quietly, hoping he'd hear the rest of her plans before she realised he was there.

He wasn't disappointed.

'Len,' she continued, 'you go to bed now, then take over from Paul at six. We have to do the town clinic, but we might be able to cut it short. As soon as we finish the fellow with the leg, I'll take over from Jazzy at the hospital, she and the boss can have a sleep, then he and Jazzy can go to town late morning. Paul will be back up to take over from me at midday, then, if these two are OK, Lurie might sit with them in the afternoon and we'll sort the rest out from there.'

She should be looking pleased with herself for marshalling her limited troops so efficiently, but he could see a frown pleating her eyebrows and almost see the waves of anxiety flowing from her body.

The anxiety and his own disquiet that she should be upset touched him simultaneously, and he spoke before remembering he'd been a silent observer.

'Are you still worrying about that boy?'

'Of course I am,' she sighed. 'It's been over an hour and Carl and Ben aren't back.'

He knew there was no way she'd accept a hollow reassurance, and a hug was hardly appropriate—or advisable—in these circumstances, so he shrugged and asked if she was ready to help him with a plaster.

'The X-ray shows two breaks, tib and fib, low down,' he told her when she followed him back into the makeshift operating theatre. 'It's the kind of break we'd plate and pin if we had the necessary equipment, but we should be able to make do with a plaster. I'll start with a back slab, under his foot and up to just below the knee, hold it there with bandages, then X-ray again in a few days to see if the bones are aligned.'

She'd picked up the X-ray film from a small table by the wall, and held it in front of the lamp, seeing the injury for herself.

'Will you do a full plaster later on?'

'Probably,' he told her, soaking the prepared bandages in a bucket of water preparatory to setting them in a curve under the young man's foot and around the back of his injured leg.

Ellie set the X-ray down and came to help him, supporting the leg and patting the plaster into place as he applied it. He could feel the heat of it in his hands as it set, and the heat of desire for this woman in his body.

Two months! He'd go berserk. Somehow he had to get past this obsession with Ellie and concentrate solely on the mission.

Maybe he could send her back on the plane when it returned the week after next.

He had no idea where the notion had sprung from, but it had merit. He'd even have a reason for dismissing her from the team—disobeying orders.

That was if she went through with the insane idea of contacting the rebels.

Or perhaps he could seduce her with deep, drugging kisses and soft, sensual caresses, then bring up the no-fraternisation rule.

His body seemed to find this a most thought-worthy option...

'Are you sure it should go up that high?'

He looked down at what he was doing—plastering the patient's thigh—muttered something inaudible and forced his thoughts back to the job.

'Keep the bandages fairly firm,' he told Ellie, as she began to wind the long strips of crêpe bandage around the plaster. 'We want to immobilise the leg as much as possible without compromising the blood supply to his foot or risking compartment syndrome if there's more swelling.'

They were settling him on to a stretcher in the former living room of the main house when the roar of the silencer-less old car signalled the return of Ben and Carl.

Nik saw the frown disappear from Ellie's face and a slight smile lighten her features. He followed her out onto the veranda, where darkness prevented him seeing that smile disappear as she turned from one man to the other.

'Where's the boy?' she asked immediately, and Carl lifted his shoulders and held out his hands in a classic gesture of helplessness.

'He wasn't there, Ellie. He'd disappeared.'

'He can't have disappeared. He was trapped. If we couldn't get him out, how could he have got out alone? And if he did, he can't have gone far. He might have been concussed—disorientated. He could be lying injured somewhere in the jungle.'

'We searched,' Ben said tiredly. 'And he didn't get out alone. Carl's sure the steering-column had been moved.'

He turned away from her towards Nik, who was standing in the shaft of dim light thrown from inside the house.

'Talk to you a minute, boss?'

Ellie stepped towards the hapless cook.

'What do you want to tell Nik that you can't tell me? Did you find the boy? Was he dead?'

Nik cut her short, wanting to save her grief—to let her down easily—but knowing nothing short of a direct order would divert her from demanding answers to her questions.

'Jasmine needs to sleep. Ellie, you go and relieve her. I'll see you when I've spoken to the men. Ben and Carl, let's go down to the kitchen. I don't know about you guys, but I could use a sandwich and a hot drink. We'll send something over to the hospital for you, Ellie.'

He ushered the two men out the door and walked away before Ellie could argue with him. He hadn't wanted to speak so abruptly to her, especially not in front of the others, but he knew, having been reminded of her job, her strict work ethic would have her heading for the hospital, no matter how furious she was with him.

Ellie stomped towards the hospital. She was glad he'd ordered her back to work. It had reminded her of things she'd been tending to forget since she'd been thrust into the maelstrom of emotion caused by Nik's arrival.

But her heart ached as she thought about the child with the huge, frightened eyes, and fear for him followed her as she made her rounds. Nik came as he'd promised, but could only repeat what the two men had already said—that it looked as if someone had rescued the boy. And because Nik looked so exhausted, she didn't nag about searching, simply accepted his words.

'I'm sorry,' he added, hesitating in front of her, so close she could see his chest move as he breathed and imagined she could see a pulse throbbing in his neck.

'I know,' she said, bending her head so she didn't have to look at any part of him—hoping not seeing him might make her feelings for him go away.

They didn't, but he did, touching her lightly on the shoulder as he whispered a husky good-night.

Not that she'd given up on the boy. Her mind, eager not to think of Nik, circled ideas for his salvation—throwing up suggestions from the ridiculous to the impossible.

With dawn came a decision. She'd contact Maze at breakfast-time and talk to her about the problem. Maze knew everyone in the camp. She might even know the missing boy. Maze would think of something.

Relieved to be able to shelve it for a while, Ellie started on the morning ablutions routine, helping patients who were awake and mobile to the showers, bathing little Josie herself, then changing the dressing on her head.

The little girl was doing well, and gratitude for this one life saved lifted a little of Ellie's depression over the missing boy. She was tending Millie, bathing the sores on her back, when Nik came in, carrying a breakfast tray.

'Carl's bringing the others,' he said. And though Ellie's heart beat faster, just hearing his voice, she hid her reaction, fussing over details as she finished bathing Millie. 'I told him to set them down at the end of the corridor and you'd sort things from there.'

Ellie nodded, passed Millie her meal, then set Josie's porridge on the little metal locker between the beds.

'I'll feed Josie, you see to the rest of the patients,' Millie offered.

Ellie was torn between gratitude that Millie would lighten her workload and dismay that she now had no excuse to linger in the room and would have to accompany Nik out into the corridor.

Out into the danger zone of closeness!

'Thanks for bringing over the meals,' she said, talking work to keep her mind off other things, 'but if you're going to do the town clinic later, you should be sleeping.'

'I'm going up to the house now. I grabbed an hour earlier, then had to check on the shoulder patient. Another couple of hours and I'll be OK.' He tucked the empty tray under his arm and looked down at her, his eyes, dark-shadowed by tiredness, probing hers, as if seeking an answer to a question not yet asked.

Heat shimmied deep inside her, sending tendrils down her legs and up to coil around her heart and lungs. Desperate to escape the effect just standing near him had on her, she asked a question of her own—the one that had haunted her during the night.

'Why were the men so sure the boy escaped?'

He reached out his hands, propping them against the wall, effectively trapping her between his arms.

So much for escaping the effects of his proximity!

'The big man was shot, Ellie,' he said quietly. 'And it could have been a bullet, possibly ricocheting off something, that broke the other man's collarbone and drove the bone fragment into his artery. Maybe it wasn't a simple accident. Maybe it was an ambush, the driver shot and the vehicle then going out of control down the slope. Why? We don't know.'

He raised one hand to brush his knuckles across her cheek.

'But we do know that there must have been other people around—at least one person to do the shooting. Carl's certain the steering-column trapping the boy had been shifted to release him, Ellie. He's not lost and alone out there in the jungle.'

Ellie knew she should feel relief, but this new knowledge—and her response to knuckles brushing against her cheek—made her feel worse.

'He might have been taken as a hostage,' she muttered, clinging desperately to the conversation about the boy. 'Whoever has him might kill him!'

Nik sighed.

'They might—there's a war going on—but most people don't make war on children. Think positive: maybe they won't kill him. Maybe they'll look after him. Maybe, even, you stubborn woman, he was one of their own, which would explain the ambush and shooting.'

Then, apparently forgetting—again—both the no-fraternisation rule and his engagement, he leaned forward and stopped any further argument with a kiss.

Exhaustion dogged Nik's footsteps as he made his way back to the main house. Carl and Ben had brought the dead men's bodies back in the car, and had laid them out in what had been the old cold room off the kitchen. Although there wasn't enough power to keep it running for this purpose, it was insulated so it was cooler than the outside temperature.

He'd get Arwon to identify the men, inform their families and arrange for their burials—

when and if he found Arwon. He checked on his two patients in the living room, then, knowing he'd be no use to anyone without sleep, he went to bed. It seemed only minutes later he was awoken, though a quick glance at his watch told him he'd slept for close to four hours.

Shaking his head in an attempt to clear it, he made his way out to the front veranda, where about six young soldiers were all talking at once, their voices getting louder and louder as they tried to convey something—the happenings of the night?—to Arwon.

Nik added his own explanations, finishing with, 'We've two injured men here. You can see them now if you like, then I'd like you to identify the two who died.'

'Only four in the car?' Arwon asked, and suspicion, lurking in Nik's mind since he'd confirmed the big man had been shot, nodded, hoping a gesture wasn't quite as much of a lie as the spoken word.

He pulled on some clothes while Arwon visited his two men, then escorted the local leader down to the cold room to see the bodies. Arwon asked questions about the accident, and Nik answered, skirting the issue of the missing fifth occupant of the vehicle, although he wasn't sure why he hadn't come clean about the boy.

Because Ellie had been so upset about the child?

He hoped not. If he began functioning on the basis of her feelings, they could all be in trouble. Though, now he came to think of it, it wasn't like Ellie to be so stressed over an unavoidable situation. She could be as cool, as compassionate and yet as detached as he was himself.

And if she'd changed in some way—beyond the physical act of cutting off her hair—would that explain the explosive reawakening of his attraction towards her?

And why had she cut off her hair?

'The big man is my uncle, the younger one a soldier. I will arrange for both their burials.'

Arwon's statement broke into Nik's thoughts.

'Thank you,' he said, because there wasn't much else to say, although, when he thought about it, surely Arwon should be thanking him for the team's rescue efforts.

'We will be leaving the camp when it is done,' Arwon told him, as they walked back to the main house. 'I will make sure people visit the wounded soldiers.'

'Not more fighting, Arwon!' Nik begged, although he knew it was none of his business.

Arwon shook his head.

'We move into town. Protect the people who are rebuilding there. You are safe enough here now the people have accepted you.'

Nik didn't find this explanation reassuring—or even totally believable—but he went along with it, wishing Arwon luck, saying he hoped to see more of him in town.

Were they being left to the mercy of the rebels? Because they'd lost a child neither of them had seen fit to mention?

Should he have listened to Ellie's pleas and made sure someone had stayed with the child?

Nik lifted his hands and rubbed them tiredly over his face, as if the physical cleansing action might wash away his thoughts. Whatever happened would happen. He couldn't replay yesterday in the hope of getting a better outcome. What he could do was grab a bite to eat, find the large and cheerful Jasmine and head for town himself.

Maybe she'd pick up some news of what was happening as she chatted to the clinic patients.

Ellie worked through until midday, visiting the young girl in the far container, pleased with the state of her wounds and the attitude of the women who cared for her. They were vociferous in their disapproval of the 'play' and had begun organising themselves to supervise the children.

Marnika, their very pregnant patient, wasn't smiling, but she was looking less emaciated, and as Ellie passed the container where Maze was coaxing her new friend to have just one more sip of milk, the woman nodded at Ellie as if acknowledging the woman who was forcing her to live.

The toddler played happily with other children not far from the two women. He looked so well fed and cared for, Ellie knew he was much loved. If the woman had such love to give that little boy, surely she'd find a little more in her heart for the new arrival.

'Though,' Ellie said to Paul, who'd come to take her place at the hospital, 'you could hardly blame her if she hated it. Innocent of wrongdoing though it is, it will always be a reminder of what happened to her.'

'Let's worry about now, not tomorrow or the next day,' Paul reminded her. 'Before you sleep, could you look in on the soldiers? The one with the wounded shoulder is still heavily sedated, but the other one is moaning and groaning and Len's not sure if it's real pain or the guy's a wuss.'

'He's only young, and a broken leg *is* very painful,' Ellie said. She walked across to the house, entering the room where Lurie had taken over from Len, watching the two soldier patients.

'His leg hurts,' Lurie told her, and Ellie knelt beside the boy, unwrapping the bandages so she could see the leg itself.

It was puffed up from the knee to the tips of his toes, and an unhealthy bluish-purple colour. She pressed her fingers against the skin of his foot and saw the white indentations left in the accumulation of fluid beneath the skin.

'Has he had it elevated?' she asked Lurie, who shrugged and explained she'd only taken over from Len half an hour earlier.

'Let's elevate it now,' Ellie suggested, grabbing some cushions from a sofa that had been pushed against the wall. She lifted the leg, holding the cast beneath it, then placed it gently on the cushions.

'We should put a cold pack on it as well,' she said, thinking they should have thought of this the previous night, though they'd all been tired and their efforts had been concentrated on the other patient. 'I'll slip across to the kitchen and see if Ben can rustle up some ice.'

What else? she wondered as she made her way back to the house, a small bucket of ice in her hands. Diuretics? Nik would know, but Nik wasn't here. Should she rewrap it or leave it free? With sprains and strains, compression from a bandage reduced swelling, but in this case, where the cast made full compression impossible, she didn't know that wrapping it would help.

She showed Lurie how to pack the ice so it wouldn't burn the boy's skin, left the leg unbandaged and went to bed. Nik would know what to do when he returned, and she doubted anything too drastic could happen in the meantime.

If you didn't call delivering a baby drastic!

She'd barely lain down when Maze's daughter arrived, summoning Ellie to see Marnika who was now, impossibly surely, in an advanced stage of labour.

'Has she been complaining of pains?' Ellie asked Maze, refusing to believe a woman could have gone from nothing to 'about to give birth' in such a short time.

'She doesn't complain, doesn't talk much, just watches her little one,' Maze said, as the woman, squatting on the ground with two other women supporting her back, shrieked and strained, and delivered into Ellie's hands a small but perfectly formed baby girl.

'It's a girl,' she said—or hoped she said—in Erirekan.

The woman looked away, but Maze picked up a towel from the pile Ellie had grabbed and wrapped the baby in it, crooning to the squalling infant until it quietened in her arms.

The two women who'd supported the patient during the birth waved Ellie away, indicating they'd take over the final stage and total care of her patient. Knowing there could be rituals or customs she didn't understand, she left them to it, crossing the room to where Maze held the baby.

'Could you keep the baby here, Maze?' she asked quietly, pleased Maze understood English so this conversation didn't have to be in Erirekan. 'I can bring you feeding bottles and formula and sterilising powder—all you'll need—but I think the baby would be better here than at the hospital.'

'Near the mother?' Maze guessed, and Ellie nodded.

'She might kill her.'

'Oh!' Ellie hadn't considered that—having simply thought that if the baby was about, the mother might take an interest in it, which would be the first step towards a possible bonding. 'Do you think she would?'

Maze looked from the woman, who was now sleeping on a pallet of grass and rags in a corner of the room, to the baby, then back to the woman.

'I don't think so. She loves the little boy so much, she not harm a child.'

'Would you be willing to do it? Babies are a lot of work.'

'You're telling me?' Maze said. 'I had nine. Arwon—he's mine.'

'Arwon's your son? Why didn't you say? Why didn't he say?'

'He said not to say. He said it's war and dangerous to say, but he made me come and live here.'

Ellie shook her head, realising how much she didn't know about these people among whom she worked. She didn't probe further, but promised Maze she'd gather up some things and bring them back. She wasn't entirely happy about leaving a newborn in the makeshift housing of a shipping container. Nurses who'd only ever worked in hospital situations would be horrified—and, now she came to think of it, she hadn't even done an Apgar on the baby, though

she doubted this lapse would make much difference to the baby's life.

Because their mission was to mothers and
children, they had ample supplies of formula—
lactose-free because lactose intolerance was
common in island communities—also bottles,
sterilising equipment and tablets, and even some
packs of disposable nappies, though most of the
babies she'd seen around the camp didn't wear
anything on their little bare behinds.

The choice would be up to Maze as she was
caring for the little girl. The one thing Ellie
didn't want to do was make the infant seem
even more alien to her mother, and slapping a
pristine white, plastic-coated disposable around
its tiny bottom might do that.

She packed what Maze might need into a
plastic crate and carried it across to the container. Once there, she showed Maze the formula, and how to mix it with water from the
bottle.

'When you empty the bottle, take it to the
kitchen and get Ben to boil water to refill it,'
she said.

'Water in the camp make baby sick,' Maze
agreed. 'Make me sick sometimes,' she said,
with a beaming smile down at the little one she

still held in her arms. 'Better we get her mother feeding her, no?'

Ellie smiled, pleased she and Maze were on the same wavelength.

She said goodbye and made her way back to the house, determined to go to bed before another crisis occurred to keep her from sleeping.

No crisis, but no bed either. A tall Erirekan was asleep in the room she'd shared with Jazzy—asleep in the one remaining bed she'd been intending to use.

'Arwon left him here to guard the soldiers,' Lurie explained, and though Ellie didn't think much of a sleeping guard, she knew they'd all had a rough night and left him sleeping.

Len was asleep in the room he and Paul shared—and in the only bed in that room as they'd taken the second one for the guy with the broken leg. Ben and Carl slept in a room off the kitchen, and that noisy, noisome place wasn't an option as far as Ellie was concerned. Which left the other bedroom at the main house—the one Jack and Nik were sharing.

It was obvious, just walking in, that this room was inhabited by men, but the sight of the two beds, each with a tidily smooth sleeping bag spread on it, was so welcoming, she didn't care if head-hunting cannibals inhabited it. She made for the nearest bed, sat down on it, pulled off her shoes and lay down.

But as she drifted into sleep she sniffed the pillow, and knew she'd chosen Nik's bed. The pillow and, now she was aware of it, the sleeping bag as well held the faint scent of the lemon soap he used, familiar not only from working with him but because he'd offered her a cake of it once when her toiletries had been stolen. As her body slowly released the tension of the long, long day, she turned on her side and, without conscious thought, gathered up the folds of the sleeping bag, holding it to her so the tang of lemon seeped into her dreams.

CHAPTER EIGHT

Don't Disturb the Nurse.

The sign, in Jack's firm hand, was taped to Nik's bedroom door when he returned from town, tired, cranky and filthy from having to change a flat tyre he suspected had been helped to deflate.

'You'd think we were the enemy,' he'd grouched to Jasmine on the way home, a statement she'd found uproariously funny.

'But we are,' she'd finally explained. 'We're strangers and, worse, foreign strangers, so it's best they treat us an enemy until they know for sure.'

'Which they should by now!' he'd muttered, then had changed the conversation, talking about the two patients who'd given Len cause for concern.

Remembering them—one of whom Nik was reasonably sure had lung cancer, the other Parkinson's disease—he sighed, read the sign again, then decided he *had* to have clean clothes. He'd go in quietly and grab some—without disturbing whichever nurse was inside.

Not that he couldn't guess. Paul, having handed over to Len at the hospital, had been entering the house when Nik and Jasmine had arrived, and he'd filled Nik in on the latest developments. Nik wasn't sure about leaving a newborn in what he considered the unsanitary conditions of a shipping container, but he understood where Ellie had been coming from.

He opened the door and stood looking at her, lying on his bed with her arms wrapped tightly around his sleeping bag. Would that he were in it!

The thought blotted out all others, to the extent he forgot about being quiet, so when he moved into the room to retrieve some gear, he tripped over Jack's duffelbag and would have pitched head first onto the floor if he hadn't reached out for the bed to break his fall.

The bed with Ellie in it.

She shot up, rubbing at her face, grey eyes wide with confusion.

'Nik?'

'Hey! Sorry! I didn't mean to wake you. You need your sleep. You never get enough sleep—always worrying about someone else or taking on another job.'

He was cross, concerned, alarmed, confused and as randy as hell—squatting on the floor by her bed, worried about standing up in case his physical state became obvious—worried about Ellie, who didn't get enough sleep, worried about KidCare, which would cease to exist if he didn't marry Lena.

What he should have been worried about was the way Ellie was looking at him. About the way she repeated his name under her breath. About the way that soft, breathy syllable— *Nik*—sneaked into every tissue in his body, lighting them with desire, tempting him beyond endurance…

Then they were kissing, and the taste of her blew worry from his mind. It was all there, just as he remembered it—honey, flowers, sweet heady wine—but most of all Ellie herself, the taste the very essence of her being.

'Ellie, love, I'm filthy, you should be sleep-ing—'

'Hush,' she said, and the sibilant whisper from her lips made him kiss her again.

They were both on the bed now, lying close together, clothes and sleeping bag rumpled be-tween them, content to feel each other's warmth—content with kisses.

And why not, when Ellie's kisses could trans-port him to some far-off realm where pain and suffering didn't exist, men didn't shoot each other and babies didn't die from preventable infections?

'I want more than kisses, Nik,' she whispered, maybe decades later, shifting her lips just enough for them to move in speech. 'But first a shower. I just flopped into bed—your bed—and really, really need a shower.'

'Me, too,' he agreed, but he couldn't let her go, recapturing her lips and murmuring endearments he knew he shouldn't use to her so hoped she didn't understand.

No, that was wrong—more than anything he wanted her to understand this wondrous love, but if he spoke of it, would she also understand it couldn't be?

'Most people will be at dinner. We could shower together,' she suggested. He could feel the heat in her cheeks and the Greek in him was glad it was a suggestion she felt embarrassed making. Glad of the innocence it betrayed, for all she'd been a married woman.

She shifted in his arms and added, 'It should be soon. I know we're not sticking to any firm timetable, but I must be due back on duty before long.'

'Not for hours,' Nik told her. 'Paul's worked out a new schedule to let you catch up on some sleep, and here I am stopping you from sleeping.'

She chuckled and snuggled closer.

'Am I complaining? Pushing you away?'

She lifted her head and pressed her lips, soft and warm as heated silk, to his, for the first time taking the initiative in the kiss-fest, demanding his response.

It was another moment of delight, though hammering in Nik's head was the knowledge that they had to talk—that the least he owed Ellie was an explanation of why a relationship between them couldn't happen.

Though he'd had relationships before and those past affairs hadn't been considered an obstacle to his marriage, so why should this—?

'Shower?' the woman in his arms suggested again, tentatively this time, trembling as she said it, and he cursed himself for letting things go this far, because now, when he said no, she would inevitably feel rejection.

He shifted so he could prop his head on his hand and look down into her face—touch the smooth tanned skin and trace the feathery brows, his own hands racked by tremors of unfulfilled desire.

'Ellie, we can't do this.'

She studied his face for a moment, then asked, 'Because of the fraternisation rule?'

'No,' he told her, though for an instant he'd cravenly wondered if he could use that excuse. 'No, it's more than that.'

He traced her profile from her forehead, along the line of her straight nose and down to lips, made fuller and reddened by his kisses. And more than anything, he wanted to have opportunities like this again—and again and again for the rest of his life—opportunities to lie beside her and trace her profile and talk.

'If KidCare is to continue, I need income from the shipping company. I've always had a share of the profits and my father was happy for me to spend it however I wished—my sisters spend more shopping for clothes than I do on my missions—but since he died...'

'Is this to do with the engaged and not-engaged conversations we've had?' she said, touching the tips of her fingers to his lips, tracing their outline so he found it hard to breathe, let alone reply.

'Yes,' he finally managed.

'You're Greek, or your family is—an arranged marriage?' she guessed, and this time he didn't bother with the word, just nodded.

'And do you feel you'd be cheating her—your fiancée—if you had an affair with me?'

He sat up and frowned down at the woman on the bed.

'What a question!' he muttered, suddenly angry and distressed but not sure why.

'It needs an answer,' Ellie said softly, sitting up beside him so they were now both perched on the edge of the bed.

'It doesn't deserve an answer,' Nik told her. 'Don't you understand? It's not to do with Lena, but to do with you. What I feel for you isn't…isn't…'

He couldn't work out what it wasn't, but ever-helpful Ellie found the words.

'An affair-type feeling?' she offered, and though it sounded terrible he found himself agreeing.

'Exactly!' he muttered. 'Even at the best of times I don't like the connotations of that word "affair". To me it always sounds a bit seedy and surreptitious.'

Ellie laughed and leaned against him, her body warm and soft—inviting…

'But, Nik, really, if you think about it, what more could there be between us? We're from two different worlds. I'm a nurse from the back blocks of Australia and you're heir to a shipping

fortune. But we're both here, and for some reason, since you arrived, all the coldness that's
been inside me since Dave and Aaron died has
melted away, and for the first time in eight years
I've remembered what it feels like to be a
woman.'

She put an arm around him and kissed him
on the cheek, as Ellie the friend had done so
many times.

'I'd like to take that feeling further, and how
better than with a man I'd trust with my life?'

'I don't believe this!' Nik stood up and glared
down at her, only with difficulty keeping his
voice to a whispered kind of roar. 'You've finally got over the death of your husband—
which, as a friend, I'm glad of for your sake—
and now you're offering yourself to the first
man who comes along. How does that fit with
the grieving you've done all these years, and the
memory of the man you so obviously wor-
shipped? What would he think of your behaviour?'

He wasn't sure why he was so indignant, or
certain it was with Ellie, not himself. For all he
knew, he might even be mad at her poor dead
husband.

He thrust his hands through his hair and took a turn around the room, trying to work out what on earth was happening. To him. To Ellie.

With Ellie...

He looked at her, sitting on the bed, head and shoulders now bowed in an attitude of utter rejection. But when she looked up, her eyes were bright with laughter and her lips trembled with it as she said, 'Would telling you I loved you make you feel better about the affair thing?'

'No!' he stormed, though inside he knew that her telling him she loved him might just break his heart. Not that it was likely—the wretched woman was teasing him.

Then, not knowing what to say, or what to do, or where to go from here, he dropped down on his knees in front of her, framed her face with his hands and drew her lips to his.

He was still kissing her when Jack, ignoring his own note, walked in.

'Just as well,' Ellie said, recovering far faster than he. 'I have to have a shower.' She stood up and moved towards the door, pausing to smile at Jack.

'Do you want a kiss as well?' she asked him cheekily. 'I'm giving them away free until ten o'clock tonight.'

As Ellie whisked out of the room without waiting for a reply, she wondered why she'd said such a stupid thing to Jack.

Because it was a night for saying stupid things?

There were levels of stupidity in what she'd said as well. Right at the top—given the current circumstances—was her prissiness in deciding she needed a shower when it had been obvious to both of them where the kisses would have led had she not interrupted things by making that suggestion.

Then suggesting the affair, which had obviously affronted Nik, though he was the one betrothed—the one who shouldn't have been initiating kisses.

The only stupid thing she *hadn't* revealed was how she felt about him. She'd asked a rhetorical question mentioning the word 'love', but that wasn't the same as explaining how she felt. Explaining how, in some mysterious manner, the emptiness within her had suddenly been filled up by him—by his presence, or by thoughts of him, dreams of him and longing for him.

Nik came at nine forty-five, with a cup of coffee and some cake Ben had made.

'Brought you supper,' he said, standing in front of her, holding the tray. They were in a small alcove at the end of the passageway, where a metal desk formed a makeshift office. 'I'd wave it but the coffee would spill,' he added, no glimmer of a smile lightening his dark features. 'It's in the nature of a white flag, you see.'

'And you're surrendering to what?' Ellie demanded, far more unnerved by this playful yet serious Nik than she'd been by the angry one earlier.

He shrugged his shoulders then, as the coffee slopped into the saucer, set down the tray.

'Not surrendering so much as apologising. I had no right to say the things I said. This new attraction— No, it's not new to me, it's always been there, but so one-sided I never acted on it. Anyway, it's thrown me. So much has happened in the last month—my father's death, my mother's and sisters' grief. My grief as well, I loved the man. Then finding out he'd left things so marrying Lena, his best friend's daughter, was the only way I could keep KidCare going...'

He threw up his arms in a gesture of total despair.

'On top of all of that, I arrive here and find you'd changed. You'd lost that long plait of hair I used to think of as a tribute to your dead husband, but with it you seemed to have cast off the "touch me not" aura you've always carried with you. There you were, as beautiful as ever, and suddenly, intoxicatingly accessible. That was not easy to accept, Ellie. Not easy at all.'

'Am I supposed to say I'm sorry now?' she teased him, her heart hammering as she learnt of feelings he'd kept hidden for so long. He'd been attracted to her for years? He thought she was beautiful? 'I thought you'd come to apologise to me, not the other way around.'

'I am apologising,' he said gruffly, 'though, you have to admit, it wasn't all my fault.'

She hesitated, knowing this was a pivotal moment—knowing she was opening herself up to a world of hurt at some point in the not-too-distant future, but, having tasted the mystery and delight of love again just from his kisses, she knew the pain would be worth it. She leaned towards him.

'Kisses are only free until ten. You've four minutes left.'

And with that she kissed him. Who cared if he *was* engaged? From what he'd said, if she hadn't been so wrapped up in her grief, the two of them might have had an affair—whether he liked the word or not—years ago, so what difference would it make to the absent Lena if they had one now instead?

Two months, that was all they had. A few days less, in fact.

He responded, growling under his breath as if he'd gone all Greek and was objecting to her making the first move—but not objecting enough to stop the kisses.

Not objecting enough to halt the flare of heat that threatened to consume them. His lips pressed against hers, seeming to drink in some essence necessary to his life, so fiercely did he kiss her. And with all barriers swept away, she responded, so in a small alcove in a run-down accommodation unit she was transported to places she'd never visited before, as if Nik's kisses were taking her on a wildly sensual journey to the bright stars he'd pointed out to her only a couple of nights earlier.

Then he drew away, speaking gruffly, hands smoothing caresses across her shoulders, the blaze of passion in his eyes denying the words he spoke.

'It's impossible. Close confines, not enough staff, the rules—impossible,' he grumbled, but Ellie could feel the heat still simmering between them, and knew nothing was impossible. Suddenly she wanted Nik as she'd never wanted anything before.

'Come with me into the hills when I go to see Rani,' she suggested. 'We'll have a night together—one night. Would that hurt anyone?'

She moved away from him so she could see his face and look into his eyes, revealing through her own the love she felt. She knew she couldn't have him for ever—but one night…

Surely that wasn't too much to ask.

Shadows chased across his face and she knew he was tempted, then he frowned and said, very quietly, 'I refuse to lose my temper with you again, Ellie, but you know you cannot go into the mountains to see that man. And how irresponsible would I be to go with you, leaving the team without a doctor when both of us are taken prisoner or killed?'

He spoke with such deadly emphasis she knew her mad idea had not only finished the kissing for tonight but had probably finished it for ever.

Thinking of the mission, of the team and of the reason they were here had re-awoken Nik's dedication to aid work, and particularly to KidCare. Ellie knew she'd lost him—though he'd never really been hers in the first place…

*   *   *

She worked through the next few hours, knowing that his final rejection of her rash idea had been for the best. As Nik had said, any kind of affair between them in such restricted circumstances would have been impossible—or shifty and dodgy and uncomfortable enough to kill any joy or pleasure being together might have brought.

And though she'd told herself she could go through with a brief affair and bear the pain of parting when it ended, deep down she suspected she'd been lying. That the pain would have been far worse than losing Dave and Aaron, although for eight long years she wouldn't have believed that possible.

But her love for Dave had been young love, and for Aaron that of a mother for her baby. Neither would ever be forgotten, secure in their own special corners of her heart and living on there and in her mind for ever.

Nik was different because mixed with love was admiration, and deep respect, and a bond of some kind that had formed and held between them from the first time they'd met.

She left her cold coffee sitting on the table and walked back along the passageway, shining her torch into each room to check on the occupants, stopping in Josie's room, because the little one was whimpering softly. She sat on the edge of the bed and lifted the little girl, rocking her in her arms, reminding herself of the fulfilment her job brought her.

'The rest is just sex,' she whispered to the now sleeping child, then she set her back on her mattress and moved on, checking the mother and baby, sleeping in the same bed now the woman's sores had healed.

What would become of them? Would they go back to the hills? Would the woman remember the way? Would she be willing to show Ellie how to get there, because although it would, as Nik had said, be totally irresponsible for them both to go, surely she could still make the journey?

Thinking positively, she headed back to the table, drank the cold coffee, ate the cake—if it was cake, it tasted most peculiar—then jotted down some notes for Paul. The woman and baby could be moved to a container—she would see Maze to find out where and who would watch over them and guide the woman through camp routine. Then the two soldiers could come down to the hospital—Carl had found an old rescue stretcher in one of the old mine storage sheds. He'd cleaned it up and it could be used to carry the men between buildings. Then the roster could return to normal.

And I'll have next weekend off, she told herself. She wasn't quite as confident about the journey now, but she knew she had to try to do something to stop the fighting before more generations of children were affected.

One part of her felt it was the right thing to do—the only thing to do—while another part suggested she didn't want to cause Nik more problems than he already had. Unfortunately, a rather strident inner voice now suggested the problems would be of his own making for forbidding her to go, but she didn't think she should listen to that voice.

The night was one of the quietest she'd had on duty, and she even put her head down on the table and dozed for a short time. But in the early hours of the morning—two thirty-eight she registered, nurses' training decreeing she automatically looked at her watch—a cry from outside made her pick up her torch. She stood at the top of the steps near the poinciana tree and shone the light around, catching a flash of movement, then, when she turned the torch back that way, the wide, dark eyes of a child.

The little boy?

'Hey!' she called softly, not wanting to frighten him, then she remembered he was Erirekan, and said hello in his own language and beckoned to him. He didn't budge.

If she moved towards him would he run away?

'Do you want something to eat?' she asked, thinking he must have been hiding in the jungle until hunger had brought him here. 'Shall I get you something?'

The boy didn't answer, remaining huddled where he was near the base of the tree. She couldn't blame him for not trusting her. Hadn't she deserted him? Talking to him all the time, Ellie came slowly down the steps. She took one step towards him and strong arms seized her from behind, a large hand clamped across her mouth smothering her cry for help.

She kicked and struggled, kept trying to yell, though it did no good. One man—no woman could be so strong—held her while another tied her arms behind her back, then caught her kicking legs and lashed them together at the ankles. A rag was thrust into her mouth and tied into place to gag her, and her first thought wasn't of the powerlessness of her position but that the rag was probably filthy and loaded with noxious germs. If her captors didn't kill her, she'd die of some unidentifiable disease.

This thought made her realise she wasn't frightened.

'We are sorry to tie you up, but you would not have come willingly. We are not going to harm you.' As the man who'd held her offered this assurance, the answer to her lack of fear clicked into place in her shocked brain. He'd been talking to her all along—in English—telling her he wouldn't hurt her. Telling her something about the boy...

'Is the boy all right?' she tried to ask, but the gag made her choke on the words.

'We will take it out as soon as we are out of the camp,' the English speaker told her.

Out of the camp? What about her patients?

Ellie tried again—to tell him she couldn't leave her patients without care. But all she did was gurgle and though she nodded her head towards the hospital, the man who held her ignored her, lifting her and slinging her across his shoulder like a roll of carpet, marching out of the camp as if he carried a toddler, not a tall, well-built woman.

They walked for a long time—or so it seemed to Ellie, jouncing about on the man's shoulder—then he set her down, holding her to keep her balanced while he undid the gag from her mouth.

Fury burst forth, though her tongue was dry and her cheeks felt bruised.

'I can't go off and leave those patients—I'm the only one on duty. The old man could light his pipe, set fire to his bed and burn everyone to death.'

'In war, people die!' the big man said, so sententiously Ellie couldn't contain herself.

'There shouldn't be a war, you stupid man. You're all one people, one nation. You've lived together for thousands of years without all this war stuff. Minor skirmishes maybe, but war with guns? It's ridiculous! And it's not getting you anywhere.' Her anger wasn't getting her anywhere either, for the man simply lifted her off the ground and dumped her in the front seat of an old Jeep. But she was so angry she could feel heat radiating from her body and couldn't have stopped venting her feelings if she'd tried. 'All you're doing is making things hard for the women and children and the old men. They've no homes, not enough food, no security. And if I'd known you were going to kidnap me, I'd have brought the photos. I want to talk to you so-called soldiers about some things. The effect of this war on Erirekan children is just not acceptable.'

She wasn't even sure they were hill soldiers who'd captured her, but though Arwon and his men had left the camp she didn't think they'd have pulled this stunt.

They drove without lights for a long time, though when they reached a place where the driver deemed it safe to turn on lights, and Ellie could read the driver's watch in the glow from the dashboard, it was only a little over an hour since her capture.

At four, in jungle so thick no light from the moon or stars penetrated it, the driver stopped the car. He got out and lifted out the boy who'd been asleep in the back seat. The big man undid the rope around Ellie's legs.

'Now we walk,' he said, and walk they did, though in her case it was more a stumble—three steps, trip, fall, be picked up, stumble forward again.

'If you untied my hands I could save myself when I fall,' she told the man who helped her up each time.

'Rani said you're a clever woman and will try all tricks,' the man said, finally confirming Ellie's assumption they were on their way to meet the rebel leader.

'Rani is my friend,' she responded. 'He will be angry when I arrive all covered in scrapes and scratches.'

She must have stumbled six more times before the man untied her arms, leaving Ellie to wonder just why he'd ever thought her having her arms free might be dangerous.

Because I can pick up a rock and hit him on the head perhaps?

Escape?

She gave the matter some thought, but she was already tired and knew she'd never outrun the other man, who simply had to put down the boy and give chase.

Besides, she wanted to see Rani. She didn't have the photos but she'd tell him what was happening—tell him all the things that had been boiling inside her since she'd seen the young girl's burns, and the way the wire had torn into her flesh...

And this way, she wasn't even disobeying Nik's orders.

Nik...

Nik didn't even know she was gone.

'Ellie's not in camp. The old man—the one in the hospital—says she hasn't done a round since two o'clock.'

Paul woke Nik with this far from welcome news, and he felt his nerves tighten, first with fear for her then, when he remembered the conversation they'd had the previous night, with anger.

No, forget the anger—Ellie might defy him and go into the hills to talk to the rebels, but she would never behave irresponsibly towards her patients. She would never, willingly, have left her post.

Fear returned a thousandfold. He was out of bed, pulling on clothes, telling Paul to organise another search of the camp, though Paul assured him people had already searched.

'Her torch was just outside the hospital—near the poinciana tree,' Paul told her, and Nik's gut knotted with anxiety.

He had to think—to get past the fact that this was Ellie missing and concentrate on getting a member of his team back safe and sound.

'You go back to the hospital. If she's been taken for ransom we'll hear from someone soon. Until then, I'll recheck the camp, and then we wait.'

And go mad from worry!

Paul departed and Nik went in search of Jack, who seemed to need so little sleep he prowled through half the night. Maybe he'd seen or heard something.

Ben also got up early to start on breakfast—but the old man said she hadn't done a round since two. Ben wouldn't start that early.

Jack was in the kitchen, and though everyone there, including the local helpers, had heard Ellie was missing, they had no clue as to what had happened to her.

'Someone must have seen or heard something,' Nik said, battling the urge to yell at them all for their uselessness, knowing it was worry for her fuelling his anger.

'I'll go and ask at the container closest to the hospital,' Jack offered. 'I know some of the women living there.'

Nik didn't ask him how he knew them—Jack always made contacts within hours of arriving in a new place.

'Is that where the woman with the new baby is?' Nik asked, thinking he should perhaps do something medical, like check both of them.

'No, they're in with Maze in the next one along,' Jack told him. 'Both doing well. Leave it to the women. It's women's business here, having babies. I'll go around the containers and talk to people for you.'

Feeling totally useless, Nik made his way to the hospital.

'Glad you're here,' Paul told him. 'Ellie left a note.'

He must have seen hope on Nik's face, for he added quickly, 'Not a note explaining where she was going, but a note about the patients we could shift today.' He passed the note to Nik. 'I've moved the mother and baby to a container and can bring the soldiers down here, but a woman has just come in and from what I can make out, there's someone very sick in one of the containers. If you stay here, I'll get Jazzy— she should be up by now—to find out what's going on. I wish I'd learned as much Erirekan as Ellie did when we were given those lessons.'

He walked away, leaving Nik looking at the writing of the woman he loved. A woman he might never see again…

Of course he would. He had to be positive. One thing he knew for certain, Ellie, wherever she was, would be positive.

Fifteen minutes later he wasn't sure he could keep up the positive. Jasmine had appeared, the big woman carrying the limp form of a girl-child.

'The burn victim?' Nik asked

Jasmine nodded. 'We thought—Ellie and I—we had beaten any infection she might have, but last night, the women tell me, the girl tossed and turned all night. The burns have become infected, Nik. The antibiotics we've been using aren't enough.'

'Put her in the room where the woman and baby were,' he said. 'I'll examine her there.'

She was conscious, and her huge dark eyes watched him fearfully. He thought of Ellie's anger that a child should be hurt this way, and put all the reassurance he could muster into his smile.

Then he lifted the soft impregnated cloth covering the burns on one hand and shook his head.

'I'll have to debride the wounds—clean away the infection,' he said to Jasmine. 'Even with a local anaesthetic it will be horrifically painful for her. I'd prefer to do it under a general. Clean them all up while she's out of it.'

Back in Vancouver, he would have taken a sample of the infected tissue, the pathology lab would have cultured it and a drug targeted specifically at the infection would have been introduced into the bloodstream. He had no lab, and not all that wide a range of drugs.

So, what was best practice without such facilities?

His mind gnawed away at the problem as he followed Jasmine to the vacant room. He was pleased to have something to push the worry over Ellie a little to one side, but the gnawing wasn't achieving much.

CHAPTER NINE

ELLIE stumbled into the clearing. She assumed the sun was up, somewhere above the canopy of the trees through which they'd hiked. Up and up they'd climbed, and though she was exhausted pride kept her on her feet. She wasn't going to let these men think they had beaten her.

'Ah, my friend!'

A man she barely recognised as Rani—bearded now and dressed in a jungle green uniform—greeted her.

'Friends don't kidnap each other, Rani,' she told him. 'They invite people to their homes. If you'd waited a few days, you needn't have gone through with this charade or used that little boy to do your dirty work. I was coming to see you anyway.'

Anger made the words sound strong, which was good because he wouldn't realise just how tired she really was.

'You were coming to see me?'

'Next weekend,' she confirmed, although she knew she might not have come at all. 'To talk about this stupid war and the effect it's having on the children.'

He seemed about to speak, but she knew if she didn't get it all said while she was still furious, she'd lose the impetus to speak to him at all. She held up her hand.

'And don't tell me war's part of life and children should get used to it. That's nonsense. This island race existed for thousands of years without the trouble that's going on now.'

The words dried up and her knees trembled with tiredness, but she held herself together, remaining stiffly upright as she glared at him.

'Next weekend might have been too late,' Rani said, and Ellie realised he probably hadn't heard a word she'd said about the war—too focused on the timing of her proposed visit.

'Too late for what?' she asked, then regretted showing interest.

'For my wife. She's having pains. She's frightened.'

Bloody hell! The pregnant wife! Rani had brought her here to deliver the baby. Please, God, let it be a normal, regular, uncomplicated delivery and both mother and child survive. Ellie muttered the silent prayer, certain that if either died, she would make a second body to be disposed of in the jungle.

'Is she in labour now?' she asked, and Rani looked at her as if he didn't understand the question.

'Is this your first child?'

He nodded.

'I'd better have a look at her. Is there somewhere I can wash my hands?'

She held out her hands towards him and saw him frown at the blood and dirt that caked them. Angrily he turned on the big man, berating him in Erirekan before leading Ellie to a roughly built shelter and showing her inside. There was a basin on a table, soap and a towel, and under the table were bottles of water.

She washed her hands and face, dried them, then washed her hands again. Rani was waiting outside.

'It was very stupid of your men to just grab me,' she told him. 'If they'd said why you wanted me, I could have brought gloves and instruments to take your wife's blood pressure and listen to the baby's heartbeat.'

Rani frowned at her.

'You would have done this if we told you why you were needed?'

'Of course I would. I'm a nurse, Rani. I don't think in terms of one side or the other but help anyone who needs help.'

He mumbled something at her, leading her towards a more substantial shelter, built of logs with fern-frond thatching.

'My wife, Ursula,' he said, introducing her to a small, slim, pale-skinned woman whose bulging abdomen seemed too heavy for her frame to support.

'Ursula?' Ellie repeated, as bemused by the woman's name as she had been by the colour of her skin.

The young woman straightened her shoulders and offered Ellie an imperious glare.

'I'm from New Zealand. I met Rani when he was studying in Wellington years ago.' Ursula spoke with the condescension of a queen to one of the lowliest of her lowly subjects. 'We were at university together.'

Ellie didn't need someone giving her attitude! As tired as she was, she launched into the attack. 'And you condone his behaviour with this stupid fighting?' she demanded.

'People like you don't realise what it's like to be robbed of your birthright,' Ursula snapped at her, and Ellie threw up her hands.

'Spare me,' she said. 'Though I don't think much of your baby's birthright, if this hidden jungle existence is all you want for him.'

Realising she was antagonising the two people who were responsible for her continued
safety, she took a deep breath and retreated.

'I'm sorry—I get cranky when I'm tied up
and slung into a vehicle, then frog-marched
through the jungle in the early hours of the
morning. Let's take a look at you.'

Ursula had giggled when Ellie had described
her journey, and suddenly looked absurdly
young. Maybe the queenly act was just that—
an act. She led Ellie through a curtain into another part of the little cabin, showing her the
pallet of fern and leaves on which they apparently slept.

'Should I lie down?' she asked, looking vul-
nerable now as well as young, and Ellie, realising she was frightened, took her hand.

'It would be best,' she said. 'But, first, tell me
how you've been feeling—what you've been
feeling—and where these pains are.'

'They're here,' Ursula said, running her hand
down the side of her swollen belly. 'And round
the back. Really strong.'

She looked at Ellie, and her eyes filled with
tears as she added, 'They really hurt!'

'I bet they do,' Ellie said, putting her arm
around the young woman and giving her a hug.
She imagined herself in this position—not only

isolated in the jungle with soldiers, but so far from friends and family she felt totally alone. 'They're probably only what we call Braxton-Hicks' contractions. It's your uterine muscles getting ready for the real contractions of childbirth.'

'So that's what real contractions will feel like?'

Ellie hesitated a moment. Could she lie?

Better not.

'Like that, only stronger—more painful, really,' she said, and Ursula promptly burst into tears.

'I don't want to do this. I don't want to have this baby,' she sobbed into Ellie's shoulder. 'I know I have to, but I want a hospital and an epidural. My sister had an epidural and didn't feel a thing.'

Ellie looked around her. She'd had some weird conversations in some very strange parts of the world, but this took the prize. A pregnant woman in a rebel camp in the jungle, demanding an epidural to get her through an impending birth. The thought brought a new wave of tiredness and a niggle of fear that, even if both mother and baby survived, Ursula might be angry enough about the pain she'd been through to demand Ellie be punished for it. She thought of Alice in Wonderland and the Queen of Hearts yelling, 'Off with her head.'

Not a comforting image!

'Let's have a look at you and see what's happening,' she suggested, and helped Ursula down onto the 'bed'.

The woman's pulse was strong, her heartbeats regular, and, as best Ellie could tell with her ear resting on the protruding stomach, the baby was also happy. That was, if what she heard *was* the baby's heartbeat. She had no way of being sure, though the beats were faster than Ursula's pulse had been.

Ellie examined the woman, but opted not to do an internal examination without gloves. It was obvious the birth wasn't imminent, so maybe she could go back to the camp, get what she needed and come back in time to be here for the birth.

'When are you due?' she asked, guessing at a couple of weeks, praying they wouldn't keep her here that long.

'Next week, by my calculation,' Ursula told her, rattling off how she'd worked out the due date. It sounded right, but first babies were often late.

'I'm going to feel the baby now,' she explained to Ursula. 'See how he or she is lying.'

'He,' Ursula told her, the queen back in control of herself. 'It has to be a he.'

Oh, great, Ellie thought. I deliver a girl and it's the 'off with her head' scenario again.

But as she pressed her fingers against the woman's stomach she forgot her own concerns. All her concern was now for her patient.

'Does he kick a lot?'

She spread her hands, palpating the belly with her fingers, hoping what she'd first felt was wrong.

'All the time until just recently. Now he only moves after I've had a pain.'

'That's because he's complaining about the contractions, too,' Ellie told her.

No, she'd felt right the first time. The hard bit at the top was definitely a head, while his little bottom, which should have been tucked up close to his mother's diaphragm, was settling into the pelvis. Ellie couldn't tell where his legs were—oh, for an ultrasound machine!—so she couldn't tell if he was a frank breech or just an ordinary one.

This baby had got himself into the worst possible position for an easy birth and had decided to come into the world butt first.

There was an external manoeuvre she could try, to turn him around, but usually an ultrasound before such a task showed exactly where the baby was, and would also have revealed any other problem that would make moving him dangerous for either the foetus or the mother.

So—there was no ultrasound, but no way would she attempt external cephalic version without a monitor checking the foetal heart the whole way through the procedure. She'd have to go back to the camp. *And* she'd need someone to read out the foetal heart rate as she attempted the manoeuvre. Rani should be able to do it if she explained and showed him how…

Assuring Ursula everything was going well, and telling her to rest, she slipped out of the room to find Rani pacing just beyond the curtain. Taking his arm, she drew him outside, explaining that Ursula was fine, the contractions were normal, the birth wasn't imminent, but unless the baby turned himself, they might be in trouble.

'Let her come back to the camp with me,' Ellie begged him. 'She's well enough to walk back to the vehicle, and if she's at the camp, whatever happens, we can handle it. Dr Conias has arrived. He has experience in operating should she need a Caesarean—and it could all be done in completely sterile conditions.'

'You expect me to send my wife into such danger?' Rani roared.

So much for keeping the bad news from Ursula, Ellie thought as she heard the young woman calling to her husband, then saw her emerge from the hut.

'Send me away? Why? You said everything was all right.' She turned to Rani. 'You can't send me away. They'll take me, like they took Noori.'

'Noori?' Ellie had lost the thread of the conversation—which wasn't surprising as she was about to collapse from exhaustion.

'Noori's the boy,' Rani explained briefly. 'But my wife is right—sending her to your camp would be asking for her to be taken as a hostage.'

'The soldiers from the camp took Noori? As a hostage?'

'He is my second in command's son,' Rani said. 'They would have used him to negotiate.'

'Negotiate what? Peace? Would that be all bad?' Ellie knew she was too tired to really understand what was going on, but felt she had to try. Rani, however, had other ideas. He'd moved to put his arm around Ursula and was talking to her in low tones.

Ellie sat down on the ground. She was beyond caring what happened next. In fact, the way she felt she'd have welcomed the Queen of Hearts' intervention—though she'd have preferred imprisonment to losing her head. A nice jail cell where she could lie down and sleep.

Nik finished his examination of the young girl, pleased to find the cuts from barbed wire which festooned her legs were healing well.

'I'll carry her up to the house,' he said to Jasmine. 'Into the dining room. I'll need you to monitor her during the op.'

The child was a featherweight in his arms, so slight he wondered how she was bearing the pain she must be suffering. And holding her, he understood Ellie's anger that war should be a game children played.

Ellie!

He tried to close his mind to thoughts of her, but it was impossible, because this child was special to her—the catalyst for change, for the war becoming personal.

He worked with more care and precision than he would have believed himself capable of, doing it for Ellie as well as for the child. His fingers seemed to understand the need for perfection, seeming to work without orders from his mind. But he knew it was the level of concentration that gave him this illusion, a concentration so fierce he could feel his temples throbbing, and his eyes aching from the magnifying glasses he was using. The left hand was the worst affected. His mind ran through the spectrum of antibiotics he'd begged and bought from pharmaceutical companies—a cephalosporin derivative, maybe that would combat further infection. Slowly and carefully, he draped fresh, specially treated burn dressings across the raw flesh.

That's the first hurdle jumped, Ellie, he told his absent colleague as he watched the young girl regain consciousness. Because of the drugs he'd dripped into her, she'd be pain-free for some hours, and after that he'd have to try to juggle dosages to keep her pain as low as possible. Pain could be as destructive to a cure as infection.

'I can watch her,' Jasmine offered, but Nik shook his head. With the operation over, all his fears for Ellie had returned, winding tension through his body until he felt his nerves might snap.

'You rest—sleep if you can—you'll need to do the night duty at the hospital tonight. We'll cancel the town clinics until we know where

Ellie is. If Arwon's lot have taken her, team members could be in danger in the town.'

The injured soldiers had been shifted to the hospital while he was operating and the beds in the living room made up with clean sheets. Nik had no idea how or by whom—but it didn't matter. All it meant to him was that, once he was satisfied the girl was stable, he could shift her in there, where someone would watch over her for the next twenty-four hours.

She'll be OK, he told the phantom Ellie, who hovered in his subconscious no matter how hard he tried to think of other things. And I love you, he added to her, regretting he hadn't said that to her—having spoken only of attraction and the impossibility of doing anything about it.

'Tell me what this breech means—draw it for me.'

Ellie must have drifted off to sleep, sitting on the ground in the jungle clearing. She started as Rani sat down beside her, but pulled herself together to take the sharp stick he handed her.

She used a frond of leaves to smooth the damp jungle earth in front of her, and drew a picture of a womb.

'This is the normal position of a foetus,' she told him, drawing in the baby with its head down. 'The arms are crossed across the chest and the legs tucked up, the umbilical cord, which feeds the baby from the mother's blood, is between the arms and the legs.'

She drew another womb.

'Your baby—and a lot of other babies—get into this position.'

She drew him in a complete breech, arms and legs folded.

'What I can't tell by feel is whether his legs are folded like this or if they are straight up so his toes are up near his head. That's what we call a frank breech.'

'Can babies be delivered this way?'

'They can, but the birth is usually more difficult for both the mother and the baby, and if things go wrong—which can happen even when we're expecting a normal birth—it might be necessary to do a Caesarean—you know what that is?'

'Cutting the woman to remove the baby,' Rani said gloomily. 'Ursula would not like that.'

'None of us would like that,' Ellie assured him, shuddering inwardly at the thought of performing a Caesar in the jungle with whatever sharp knife soldiers carried. Images of huge bayonets flickered in her tired mind.

'So what can we do?'

'You can let me take her back to the hospital. You can come with her—and talk peace with Arwon. How will Ursula feel if she has your baby but loses its father because of some silly feud? You're an educated man—you should be helping your people progress, not putting them in danger and causing hardships for them.'

'The hill people *are* my people and they have suffered.'

'They're suffering more now. When the mine was operating, all the people shared the advantages it brought. Obviously there were troubles, but troubles should be sorted out through talk, not fighting.'

'We were talking about my baby,' Rani said stiffly. 'The politics of my country are not your concern, but my baby is.'

'You cannot separate your baby from the political situation. How can it not be affected by this war?' Ellie told him, but she went on to explain how she could try to turn the baby.

'But I need an instrument to monitor its heart rate while I do it, and gloves and a blood-pressure monitor, and I should also get surgical instruments and sterile towels and drapes in case there's trouble during birth and I have to do a Caesar.'

'You have done this kind of operation? I would have thought a doctor did it, not a nurse.'

'I've seen it done a hundred times and could manage,' Ellie assured him, though quaking inwardly at the thought. But Nik had been right. It would be disastrous for the team if the pair of them ended up in Rani's clutches, particularly if something went wrong and Ursula exacted revenge...

'We need the doctor, too,' Rani declared. 'You will write him a note, telling him what he must bring, and I will send it with men to bring him to us.'

Ellie's heartbeat tripped into overdrive but she wasn't sure if it was the thought of seeing Nik, the fact that both of them would then be captive or the relief of having someone else to take responsibility.

Then fear for Nik intruded.

'I won't write the letter,' she said, putting down the stick she'd been using to doodle triangles around her drawings of wombs and breech babies. 'The doctor is needed where he is. The baby is not due for another week. Send me back and we can both come when Ursula goes into labour.'

'Send you back? So you can guide our enemies to our camp? Never! You will write the letter as you are told. We need instruments and gloves and the doctor. You will summon him.'

'So Ursula can have your baby then all of you go on fighting? I don't think so. What if that baby is a girl? What if you're still fighting when she's ten and burns her hands and arms playing war? Do you want to bring a child into a world where such terrible things happen?'

She could feel Rani vibrating with fury beside her, and commended his restraint when he finally replied.

'My child will be a boy.'

'Boys get injured, too—or captured, like Noori. Or grow up to be soldiers and get shot,' Ellie reminded him.

It proved too much for Rani, who got to his feet and paced back and forth in front of her.

'The war will end soon—before my son is old enough to fight.'

'I've seen five-year-olds with guns, and younger children playing war,' Ellie reminded him. 'You're angry because you know I'm right. Because you know it's wrong to bring a child into a world of war. Isn't there some way you can talk to the other side? Start negotiations for peace?'

Rani walked away from her, going into the big hut.

The argument had proved too much for Ellie's fatigue. Not caring if Rani's entire army marched over her, she lay down on the ground, tucked her hands under her head for a pillow, and went to sleep.

She was woken some time later—she'd stopped checking her watch—by a smiling Ursula.

'You might know about babies but you are stupid about men,' the woman told her.

Ellie, thinking of the fiasco of things she'd made with Nik, couldn't help but agree, though she must have been talking in her sleep for Ursula to know.

'My husband will not strike a bargain with a woman. It would lower him in the eyes of his men. Anyway, we don't need your letter. I heard what you said to him and wrote down what you need. Rani told me you came from Australia and were in the class he taught in Auckland. The doctor comes from Vancouver and has just recently arrived.'

Ellie wasn't following her. She shook her head, trying to clear the fug of sleep and tiredness from her brain, but finally had to admit defeat.

'I haven't a clue what you're talking about, Ursula. But as long as you're in such a good

mood, maybe you could tell me where the toilet
facilities are in this place. And I'd like a proper
wash. And some clean clothes.'

As she looked at the tiny woman, she knew
borrowing clothes was out of the question.

'Perhaps a length of material I can wrap
around me as a sarong.'

Ursula was frowning at her, making things on
the wash and clothes fronts seem unlikely.

'You don't want to know what we've done?'

'Not particularly,' Ellie told her, as the need
for privacy—even a bit of jungle on her own—
became pressing.

'Well, I'll tell you,' Ursula announced tri-
umphantly. 'We have sent a message to the doctor—I wrote it myself—asking for the things
you said, and telling him you're tied up without
food and water until they come—and he comes
with them. And I signed it with your name.
Men's and women's writing might look different, but he will not know your writing well
enough to doubt the letter came from you.'

How true, Ellie thought bleakly, but Nik still
won't come. He wouldn't worry about putting
himself in danger, but he is too conscientious to
leave the rest of the team without leadership.

But she didn't tell Ursula that. Let her find
out in her own time.

'Toilet facilities?' she enquired again, and Ursula laughed.

'It's all yours—the whole jungle—but keep away from watercourses and look out for snakes and spiders.'

Ellie got to her feet and glared at the pregnant woman. She was willing to bet her favourite boots Ursula didn't use the jungle.

Though once in the jungle, could she skirt the rebel hideout and make her way back to the mine site?

The thought boosted her flagging morale as she picked her way a few minutes later out beyond the hut where she'd washed, looking anxiously about for snakes and spiders, thinking of the strange way the world worked, that a woman with a university education had thrown in her lot with a rebel in a small island state and was now about to give birth in such primitive circumstances.

A brief foray into the jungle convinced her she'd be lost before she made it around the rebel stronghold, so she negotiated her way through swinging vines that scratched her skin and stinging leaves that burned like flame, back to the camp where she poured clean water from a bottle into the basin, stripped off her clothes and had a proper wash.

Ursula hadn't come up with anything in the way of clothing, so Ellie wrapped the rather grubby towel around her body and went in search of some, barging into Ursula's hut with only a token call of warning. Hadn't these people, by their behaviour, forfeited their right to small courtesies?

'You can have these trousers of Rani's and a singlet,' Ursula told her, handing her this meagre outfit. Rani was nowhere in sight, so Ellie slipped off the towel and, praying the underwear she'd washed would dry soon, pulled on Rani's trousers. She could tell from the stiffness they were clean—for which she was inordinately grateful—and the singlet hid her nakedness although it stretched across her bust and made her look positively Amazonian.

'Have you got a belt?' she asked, clutching the trousers around her waist.

'Prisoners are not allowed belts,' Ursula told her, and Ellie felt the pent-up fury from her capture and ordeal come together in a fiery explosion.

'Bloody hell, Ursula, prisoners aren't allowed belts in case they hang themselves. I could hang myself in the jungle on any of those trailing vines—but it would be by accident, not on purpose. I didn't come of my own free will, but now I'm here I'm a nurse and my duty is to help you.'

It was obvious Ursula didn't believe a word she said, so Ellie wasn't surprised when she repeated, 'You cannot have a belt,' and walked back into the room she and Rani used as a bedroom.

Ellie stomped away, wondering where she'd find a belt. She didn't wonder long. If the vines that hung from every tree were tough enough to use to hang herself, a baby vine would be good enough for a belt.

She approached a young soldier, lolling against a tree across the camp from the big hut, and asked in Erirekan to borrow his knife, pointing to the sheath hanging from his belt.

The young man straightened up and was about to hand it to her when the big man who'd carried her from the camp came from nowhere, roaring at the lad, apparently about his stupidity.

'Oh, cool it, mate!' Ellie told the big fellow. 'I don't want to escape or knife someone—I need a belt.'

She held out Rani's trousers to show him the problem, then, remembering she wasn't wearing underwear, clutched them close again.

'Ah, a belt!' The big man laughed, and, taking out his own knife, headed into the undergrowth. Seeking around at the base of the big trees, he finally found what he was looking for and returned with a length of thin, green, pliable vine for Ellie. She put out her hand to take it, but he waved her away, using the sharp knife to skin the vine.

'Otherwise the prickles tear your skin,' he said, and Ellie felt tears smart in her eyes at this surprising show of kindness.

She looped the vine through the tabs on Rani's trousers and tied it in front, reminding herself it was normal—but dangerous—for hostages to become dependent on their captors. And here she was, not yet twenty-four hours into being a captive and feeling weepy over a small act of kindness.

CHAPTER TEN

NIK was sitting by the young girl. He'd slept through the afternoon and come back on duty after dinner. Len was in the hospital, with orders not to go outside for any reason. Jasmine would work days until the crisis was resolved and Ellie returned to them.

The man who came must have been watching the camp for some time because he found Nik with no trouble, walking soft-footed into the house when everyone not on duty had gone to bed. He handed Nik the note then sat down, cross-legged, on the floor by the door.

Heart pounding in his chest, Nik opened the dirty piece of paper, and read the words. *Woman about to give birth, baby in wrong place, need gloves, instruments for operation maybe, epidural and thing to measure baby's heart. Come soon, please, Nick. Ellie.*

'Epidural!' Nik muttered to himself, wondering what jungle rebel might have heard the word, let alone known how to spell it. He'd known immediately Ellie hadn't written the letter because, pathetic though it might be—even in his own mind—he'd taken the note she'd left for Paul and had it folded in his breast pocket. Ellie's writing was like she was—upright lines and bold strokes. This was pretty writing—more like a woman's than a man's. In fact, now he looked at it again, he was certain it had been written by a woman. No man would make the dots over the 'i's into little heart shapes.

He tried to think what Ellie had told him about the rebel leader. He'd been desperate to get back! She'd told him why, but...

The anxiety he felt for Ellie was currently making thinking difficult, so recall was an effort. A wife! Rani had a wife—a pregnant wife. First baby! An epidural?

And in spite of the fear he held for Ellie's safety, and not knowing she'd been tickled by the same idea, he smiled at the image of a woman in a rebel camp, demanding an epidural during childbirth.

But the smile didn't last long, too many fearsome thoughts following the light-hearted one. Why *hadn't* Ellie written the letter?

Because she couldn't? Because she was dead?

He glared at the messenger.

'Where is my nurse?' he said, and was infuriated all over again by the man's casual shrug. It was obvious he didn't understand English, though he pointed at the letter as if to say it should explain all.

The young girl was asleep and, though she was restless, Nik felt he could leave her for a few minutes. Though not with the rebel soldier in the same room.

He stood up, grabbed the man and ushered him out of the room, steering him towards the room where Jack slept. The rebel must have objected to this treatment, for he pulled a gun and held it pressed against Nik's ribs.

'*Ise vlakos!* You ignorant child!' Nik fumed, ignoring the pressure and explaining to Jack what was happening.

'I've got to get back to the girl. Wake Jasmine for me and send her into the living room so I can ask this guy some questions. I need to know if Ellie's still alive, then I'll do a trade. Myself for Ellie.'

Jack began to argue, but Nik was already walking away, the rebel with the gun accompanying him.

Not very efficient terrorists, Nik thought. Why hadn't the rebel marched his hostage at gunpoint to wherever they wanted him to go?

He shook his head and sat down again beside the girl, waiting for Jasmine—waiting for answers.

'He says Ellie is alive, she wrote the letter,' Jasmine translated, fifteen minutes later.

'She didn't write the letter,' Nik told her. 'It's not her writing.'

He waited while the pair gabbled backwards and forwards, the rebel waving his hands to illustrate his points, Nik wondering what English sounded like to those who didn't understand it.

'He says she's definitely alive because she's wearing a tree around her waist.' Jasmine looked confused. 'The language isn't the same, just similar,' she added. 'There must be another word they have that's like tree. I mean, she can't be wearing a tree around her waist, can she?'

Unless she's tied to one, Nik thought grimly, thinking he should stop arguing and go with the soldier, if only so he'd have the satisfaction of ripping Rani's head off his shoulders.

'Tell him I will go when they bring Ellie back. He must go back to Rani with this message, that they can have me instead of her.'

'But—' Jasmine began, and he could guess the protest she was about to make. Jack would echo it, and go on about responsibility, but Nik had realised his life would be worthless in a world that no longer held the woman he loved. Whether they ended up together or not, he couldn't go on living if there was the slightest chance of saving her and he turned it down.

'Tell him!' Nik said, a new possibility percolating in his head.

Jasmine spoke again while Nik watched the soldier closely, seeking some reaction.

The soldier pulled out his gun, pointing this time at Jasmine, and Nik cursed again. He'd lost the bluff and had now put Jasmine in danger.

His mind throwing up a million thoughts a second, he rummaged through them, seeking a solution, but when it came it was from an unexpected source. The young girl, who'd been sleeping since the operation, must have opened her eyes and seen the soldier with the gun. She screamed, a high-pitched noise so eerie in its tone they were all startled and shocked. The soldier turned the gun towards the girl and Nik kicked out at his hand, knocking his arm upwards so the bullet, no doubt fired by accident, went harmlessly through the ceiling.

Jack came running, but Nik had already grabbed the gun and now held it on the soldier.

'Take his knife, Jack, and check for other weapons. Jasmine, tell him again he is to go back to his leader and say I will go with him when Ellie returns to the camp. Tell him we'll pack some food for him to take back to the camp. When you've finished talking, I'll take him down to the kitchen myself.'

Nik left the room, heading for his bedroom, while Jasmine was still speaking to the now cowed man. Nik returned as she was finishing and led the man across to the kitchen, giving him a soft drink and a bun, indicating he should eat, while Nik packed up some food. He put tinned stuff and potatoes they'd bought from the locals and some chocolate, of which there was an abundance in the camp pantries, into a sack and handed it to the man, then he led him back to the road and watched him make his way out the gate.

'Do you think Rani will release Ellie?' Jasmine asked, and Nik, feeling the adrenaline still pumping through his body, couldn't lie.

'She might not be alive to be released,' he said. 'Go back to bed, both of you. We might all think better in the morning.'

Ellie, asleep on the ground outside the washroom hut, heard the commotion, but was too tired to even think about what it might mean. Her own shirt had dried and she was wearing it and using Rani's singlet as a pillow. Now she pulled it over her head to block out the noise and drifted back into a dream where she and Nik were lost in the jungle. She was kicked awake by one of her captors.

'Rani want you,' the man said, and when Ellie failed to respond he kicked her again.

She lashed out with her legs, catching him high up on the thigh, sorry it hadn't been a bit higher. Then, not wanting him to take revenge, she scrambled to her feet and tightened her vine belt—she'd stuck with Rani's trousers as they provided warmth for her legs at this surprisingly cool altitude.

Rani arrived.

'You must write a letter to that stubborn man, telling him he has to come.'

'I can write the letter but I can't make him come,' Ellie told him. She looked at the travel-weary, woebegone-looking man who'd been the emissary and, though part of her was glad Nik hadn't given in to the rebel's pressure, another part felt saddened that he hadn't wanted to mount his white charger and come galloping to her rescue.

Of course he wouldn't have done that, she told herself. That would only have put two of them in danger.

'Well,' Rani was saying, and Ellie couldn't remember what they'd been discussing, 'you will write the letter?'

'I will tell him what I need to help your wife. He doesn't need to come.'

Ellie's heart felt heavy with that admission, but it was true. She would manage, and if, by some contrary twist of fate, she didn't live, she'd be far less loss to the world than Nik, with all he had to give to so many people, in so many ways.

She asked for pen and paper and sat down to write the letter, assuring Nik she was being well treated—he needn't know about the method the soldier had used to waken her—and explaining in detail Ursula's condition, and what she intended trying once she had a foetal heart monitor.

'Everything is under control,' she added at the end, hoping he'd get the message not to come.

Rani read it and, though he hemmed and hawed and looked dissatisfied with her missive, accepted it, folding it in quarters then handing it to the big man.

'Go as far as the road and find someone to carry it to the mine site. Don't be seen on the road in daylight,' Ellie thought he said, though he spoke in his native language and so quickly she might have got it wrong.

She went back to where she'd chosen to sleep—no one having offered her any other quarters—and settled back on the ground. She'd done it so often, in other parts of the world, that sleeping on the ground was no hardship. But in other parts of the world she hadn't been haunted by thoughts of Nik—and nudges of regret that she'd been so prissy as to want a shower on that one day she'd had a chance to...

Frustration dogged her dreams, with the result that by morning she was less tired but far more cranky, so when Ursula suggested they might play cards, Ellie exploded.

'You can't kidnap people and drag them into the forest and then expect them to play cards with you, as if this is some kind of holiday camp,' she stormed at the hapless Ursula.

'I thought it might help pass the time. I'm sick of being pregnant, and too tired to do anything, and you must be getting bored...'

She looked dejectedly up into Ellie's face, and Ellie felt her bad mood slipping away.

Not right away, though.

'I won't play cards with you,' she said, 'but I'll sit and talk.'

She dropped, cross-legged, to sit beside the other woman.

'What on earth were you thinking, coming to live in the jungle like this?'

'I won't talk if you're going to be mean to me,' Ursula said, petulance returning to her voice. 'Anyway, Rani wasn't living in the jungle. He was in the government, high up and important, and we had a house in town.'

Ah! thought Ellie. Maybe this talk isn't such a bad idea. She stood up again.

'What if I make us a cup of tea and we get comfortable? I'd really like to hear about your life, and Rani's.'

And somewhere along the line try to talk some sense into you…

Nik checked that all his staff members were where they should be, then went over his plan one more time. He'd wait until dark then, using the hand-held tracking device, follow the signals he hoped the bug, pushed hastily into a slightly bad potato, would send out.

He'd been given the bug and tracking device by an American soldier in Afghanistan, who'd taken it from rebel forces. Nik had carried it with him more as a memento of his time in that country than something he might ever need to use.

He just hoped they had plenty of food in the camp and would discard the bad potato, rather than boiling it up, bug and all, to eat.

As long as they didn't eat it tonight, he'd be OK.

He went over the timetable he would leave for Paul, so the shifts would be covered, then he checked on the young girl, smiling when he saw how well she was doing—her temperature down to normal, her wounds healing.

Down in the container homes, Maze reported that Marnika, the woman who'd had the baby as a result of her rape, was now giving advice on how Maze should be looking after the baby, and had even, this morning, when Maze had deliberately spilled the formula she'd mixed, held the baby to her breast and fed it.

So he'd have two good news stories to tell Ellie when he rescued her, he thought, refusing to countenance the fact she might not be alive to rescue.

It was a long, long day, made longer by the fact he had to keep pretending life was going on as usual. The staff were all distressed, though he'd shot enough black looks at them for them to stop discussing Ellie whenever he was near. And for some reason Arwon and his boys had returned and were patrolling around the boundaries of the camp. Nik assumed they'd heard about Ellie's disappearance and, maybe feeling guilty for abandoning the medical team, they were now making a show of their protection.

'We carry on as usual,' Nik told his team. 'Ellie will be back before long.'

Though he knew Rani wouldn't let her go because, once she was back in camp, there was no reason for Nik to take her place. Nik was reasonably sure a rebel leader wouldn't put his trust in a stranger's honour, neither could he be sure his men would have the ability to make a successful exchange.

Which was why he, Nik, was going to rescue Ellie tonight.

Fear tightened his stomach—not fear for his own safety or even his own life, but fear for what he might find. But he had to hide it, and hide his anticipation as well. The team must continue to function normally, and once he was gone Jack and Paul would see everything ran smoothly until he and Ellie returned.

The luminous dial on his watch told Nik it was after midnight, and instinct told him he was lost, but the bug kept calling to him, so somewhere, ahead of him in this terrible tangle of vicious plants that trapped and tripped and scratched at him, the woman he loved was waiting.

At least being alone in the jungle gave him time to think. Ellie's disappearance had ripped open his heart, causing such pain he knew he not only had to find her but had to keep her. He'd talk to Lena, see if they could reach a compromise. She could have his share of the company, though his mother and sisters must continue to receive their incomes from it. He was reasonably certain Lena wasn't any keener to marry him than he was to marry her, so maybe he could reach another compromise—that she keep funding at least the clinics he'd set up in Athens and Vancouver.

As far as KidCare was concerned, he'd just have to put in what he earned as a specialist and fundraise for the rest he'd need. He'd have to live cheaply, but at least Ellie wouldn't be able to throw that argument about them being from two different worlds at him again. He'd be poor financially, but rich in love.

As the frond of a fern slapped his face, he wondered if he wasn't getting a little ahead of himself here. He wasn't even certain Ellie loved him.

Certainly didn't know if she'd be willing to tie herself to him for the rest of her life.

To him and his ideals...

Another branch smacked across his skull, but the signal was getting stronger and he knew he must be close.

Ellie was dreaming about Nik. He was calling to her, but she couldn't make her way through the jungle to where he was.

The feeling was so strong she woke up, sitting up on the ground and listening, knowing it was a dream but needing to banish it before she could go back to sleep.

The cry came again—not her name but the cry of a curlew. The cry she'd taught him when they'd been finding their way out of the old underground tank, along disused underground canals.

'It's easier than talking,' she'd said, and now, hearing the curlew, although she knew it couldn't possibly be Nik, she answered.

She heard it again, closer this time, and then, impossibly, it *was* Nik, holding her in his arms, pressing kisses on her temple, telling her he loved her and he'd be poor but would she marry him anyway, and did they need paediatricians in the backblocks of Australia...

CHAPTER ELEVEN

'OH, NIK, you stupid, stupid man. What are you doing here? You said you wouldn't come because then they'd have two of us and we'd be leaving the team without support. Oh Nik.'

Ellie clung to him, feeling the solidity of his broad chest, the strength of his arms, and all the time she was berating him she was crying at the same time, feeling the tears flowing from her eyes leaving damp patches on his cheeks.

'Did you get my note? Is that why you're here? Who brought you? Where's the big man? I was so sure you'd refuse to come—I wanted you to refuse—but Rani was reading what I wrote so I couldn't write that you weren't to come. I didn't want to put you into danger. The wretched girl's not even ready to give birth—it could be weeks.'

She felt Nik draw a little away from her, though his arms still wrapped her in a cocoon of safety.

'Note? I got one note, signed with your name but not in your writing. And who's the big man?'

'Ursula wrote the first one. She signed my name. The soldier came back and Rani made me write another one. The baby's breech, you see. The big man is the man who captured me. With a smaller man to help him. The big man is Noori's father—'

Nik sighed and stopped her words with a kiss.

'I have no idea what you're talking about, but none of it's important, Ellie,' he said, stopping the kissing because it was addictive, the drug of it so potent he'd soon forget his mission. 'We've got to go—get out of here. It's hard getting through the jungle at night but we'll be safer if we leave now.'

Though Ellie was content to kiss and be kissed by Nik for the rest of her life, there were obviously some pressing issues to discuss. 'Leave? How can we leave? I looked around in daylight and thought I'd get lost. And if we leave, who'll look after Ursula? I couldn't just abandon her here, with the baby in a breech position and no help at all if she goes into labour. She could die, Nik.'

'Are you saying you *want* to stay?'

He sounded so incredulous she had to think through what she had said.

'No, I don't,' she told him. 'Ideally, we should take her down to our camp and let her wait for the birth there, where we have everything we need to help her when the time comes, but she won't leave the camp in case she's taken hostage.'

She stopped, seeking an elusive scrap of memory.

'Can't people get some kind of guarantee of safety in wars? Do they call it safe conduct? Could we ask Arwon to guarantee that?'

'Let's go back and ask Arwon,' Nik suggested, realising his heroic efforts in finding this infuriating woman were all about to come to naught if she insisted on staying to do her duty as a nurse.

'I suppose we could, and if that doesn't happen, I can come back later, nearer her time, and bring what I'll need.'

He felt her wriggling around, snuggling closer to his body.

'Though it's almost a shame we have to go. It's nice like this, isn't it?'

He kissed her again, then helped her to her feet, and together they crept into the jungle at the back of the hut.

'How did you find the place?' Ellie asked, when they were far enough away for their voices, if they kept them low, not to carry.

Nik explained about the homing device, and Ellie congratulated him on his brilliance.

'And did you leave another bug at the mine site to guide us back, or drop breadcrumbs along the way so we could follow them?'

Nik stopped so suddenly she slammed into his back.

'What?' Ellie whispered in his ear. 'Did you hear something?'

'No!' Nik growled. 'I stopped because I'm stupid. I didn't for a moment think of how we'd get back.'

Frustrated though he was by his lack of fore-thought, he was still the leader—the rescuer—and he'd get Ellie out of this black, damp, frightening jungle if it was the last thing he did.

They struggled on, Nik pursuing a deter-minedly downhill course, working on the theory that if they kept going downhill, they'd even-tually reach the lowlands somewhere. Vines, fern fronds and palm leaves all smacked around their bodies, but they moved doggedly ahead, Nik supporting Ellie as much as he could, her silence suggesting she was close to exhaustion.

Finding the road was an accident, but once on it everything became easier. It was little more than a track, but it was better than battling through the jungle, and they walked briskly along it, hand in hand, not talking much but content in each other's company.

Nik thought of all the things he wanted to tell Ellie, but he sensed she was tired and knew they would keep. For now it was enough he'd found her, and that her hand clung to his as they walked. Then ahead he saw a patch of less dense darkness, and his heart grew lighter, knowing they must be nearly back in the lowlands.

'Have a nice walk?'

The voice boomed out of the darkness to one side of the road, and though Ellie yelled, 'Run', it was impossible. Strong hands seized them, turned them around and marched them back up the road.

'I should have remembered,' Ellie said, her voice breaking with tiredness and defeat. 'The big man took the second note. It would have been daylight when he reached the lowlands and he's waited until dark to send the note and then return.'

This time, when they reached the still-sleeping camp, Ellie wasn't left to her own devices. Instead, they were shown into a small hut, one which not only had a door but, from the clink which followed its closing, a lock.

Nik felt along the walls.

'It's rough but it's solid. My guess is even a rebel army needs a lock-up for its miscreants. We're in jail, Ellie.'

He wrapped his arms around her and drew her down onto the floor, feeling in the darkness for any sign of softness.

'They don't believe in beds and mattresses,' Ellie told him, as she conducted her own search by touch in the total blackness.

'Not the first time we've slept rough, though, is it?' Nik reminded her, and he held her close, as much to ward off his own feelings of failure as to comfort her.

'I love you,' he said into the darkness, lips brushing her hair, knowledge of how he felt too strong to remain unspoken a moment longer. 'And I've worked things out. I'll let Lena have the business, on condition she keeps funding the city clinics, and we'll just have to raise the money we need for the missions like this one with functions and appeals to business people.'

'We?' she murmured, turning her head so the movement of her lips tantalised his mouth.

'You and I. There will be a you and I, Ellie.' He spoke each word as a separate entity, giving each a definite emphasis, making the simple statement a commitment.

'Do I have a say in it?' she asked, lips a breath away from his now, the non-touch even more provocative than the touch had been.

'Of course you do—you say yes. You could even say, ''Yes, Nik, darling,'' if you like, but I won't push for that right now.'

It was ridiculous, sitting in a dark, rough cell in a rebel camp, talking of the future with the woman he loved. But their situation had increased the need for commitment because, whatever happened in the future, they would have the knowledge of their shared love to give them strength and courage.

He drew her down onto the ground, lying so her body could rest against his. And though a sexual fire had burnt within him since seeing her again, that fire was tamped down now—not gone, but waiting. Tonight it was enough to sleep with the woman he loved in his arms, the warmth of her body pressed against his, the soft huff of her breathing music in his ears.

'I love you, Nik,' she whispered drowsily, and when her body relaxed in sleep, he knew she'd given him a gift beyond all the riches of a shipping company. She'd given him her trust—and beyond that again, her love.

* * *

Loud voices, yelling, then light flooding into her eyes.

'I'm sick of being woken up,' Ellie said crossly, then felt softness beneath her cheek and remembered what had happened the previous evening.

But the joy of seeing Nik—physically seeing him now daylight had crept into the jungle clearing—was swamped by worry.

'You shouldn't be here. You shouldn't have acted so rashly. It was stupid, Nik. Now they've got both of us, which was exactly what you didn't want.'

He was levering himself into a sitting position, and she knew from the aches and pains in her own body that the movement was hurting him.

'And good morning, darling, to you, too!' he snapped, rubbing at his back. 'Is it old age, or did sleeping on the ground always make me feel this bad?'

'Turn around,' she told him. 'I'll rub your back.'

Her voice was still terse, but she wasn't really angry, remembering this stupid, brave, wonderful man who'd made his way in the darkness through thick jungle to rescue her. OK, so it hadn't had quite the required outcome, but the thought had definitely been there. *And* he'd told her he loved her.

She massaged his shoulders, feeling knots of tension beneath her fingers, easing them away with her thumbs, concentrating on her task so she didn't have to think of anything else.

'Why would they have opened the door?' Nik asked, and his voice told her he was feeling less pain.

'So we can escape?' she suggested, and pressed a smiling kiss against the back of his neck.

'Don't get fresh, woman. I'm the one who had to hold you in his arms all night, fighting the urge to ravish you to within an inch of your life. One thing I can tell you—being in jail doesn't diminish the sexual urge one bit.'

They found out why the door had been opened when Rani appeared.

'So, I have the doctor for my wife. Good. I'm sorry if you were uncomfortable last night. Today my men will take you into the jungle where you can cut some palm and fern fronds to make a bed. I will have to lock you up at night, but in the daytime you can move around the camp. My wife is bathing now. In one hour you can examine her and tell me what is happening with this upside-down baby.'

'No!'

Ellie wasn't sure where the word had come from, but once said she realised it was the right one.

'No?' Rani echoed.

'No?' Nik's 'no' was even more puzzled.

'No, we won't look at Ursula. You might have taken us prisoners but you can't make us do anything. I told you earlier, I'm a nurse and as a nurse it was my duty to look after her, but I've changed my mind. And Nik won't treat her either, or help her if she has trouble with the birth.'

'But why not?' Rani asked, genuinely puzzled by this obstreperous woman.

'Because this so-called war is stupid. Because it's affecting the island's children. I don't care any more. You can kill me if you like, but unless you agree to sit down and talk with Arwon—Nik can be an observer and try to help you sort things out—I won't do anything to help Ursula.'

Pleased with the speech, Ellie was about to relax when she remembered something important.

'And neither will Nik,' she added.

Rani stared at her for a few seconds then stormed away.

'I hope you know what you're doing,' Nik said, when they were sure they were alone. 'It's all very well offering a challenge, but what if they don't accept? What if they force you at gunpoint to tend to this woman?'

'I don't think they'd do that—not after I mention to Ursula how guns can go off accidentally and what if the person holding the gun faints as the baby emerges, all covered with blood, and the gun goes off and shoots it.'

'You'd say that to a pregnant woman?' Nik said. 'Think how terrified it would make her.'

'Exactly,' Ellie said.

'So what do we do now, mastermind?' Nik teased, rubbing his hand across her short hair.

Ellie turned and smiled at him.

'I thought we might make the most of things. They've left the door open, so presumably we're free to wander around the camp. I thought I might have a wash while you use your masculine mind to figure out how we can lock the door on the inside…'

The cheeky smile was like putting a match to tinder-dry grass, and all the desire Nik had been keeping under control roared to life.

'I might come and help you clean up, *then* check the door,' he suggested, getting to his feet then pulling her up so her body rested against his. And for a little while they forgot about challenges, and shared the special pleasure only those in love could derive from kisses.

'I knew I should have gone straight to the wash house,' Ellie whispered a little later, moving away from him as someone else entered the tiny hut. 'This is Ursula. Ursula, Nik—Nik, Ursula.'

Nik nodded an acknowledgement to the woman, who was looking from one to the other and smiling brightly.

'So!' she said. 'There's something between the two of you. That's good, because now I can have Rani's men cut off small pieces of Ellie in order to force you to work.'

She was nodding towards Nik as she offered this new challenge, but Ellie answered.

'Won't work,' she said, 'because you don't know what Nik will be doing. One slip of the knife and you and the baby will both be dead. If you intend killing me—and cutting bits off me means I'll bleed to death—then he won't want to live and won't care what happens to him.'

'But he has an oath. He's not allowed to kill people.'

'That's in the civilised world,' Nik told her, unable to believe this conversation between members of the so-called gentler sex but aware he should be backing up the woman by his side. 'Out here you're operating on the law of the jungle—kill or be killed, take revenge, fight your fellow man to prove your manhood. Is this really the way you want your child to grow up?'

Ursula spat a very rude word at them and stormed away.

'Which bits do you think they might cut off first?' Ellie asked him, her voice shaky enough for Nik to have to take her in his arms again.

'Not even a hair off your head,' he told her. 'It's all a bluff.'

'So was my bold statement,' she admitted. 'You and I both know if that woman gets into trouble during childbirth we'll help her.'

'But they don't know that, so hold firm.' He kissed her one more time, then added, 'Now, what about that bath?'

Ellie led him across the clearing to the wash house. 'I seem to be the only one who uses it,' she explained. 'Maybe it was built for Ursula and she comes in earlier, but I've never seen anyone else here.'

She poured water from a bottle into the basin, showed Nik the tiny cake of soap, then moved away, suddenly embarrassed about taking off her clothes in front of him.

'I'll do my jungle walk and come back later. You have first wash,' she said, but before she could escape he caught her hand and drew her back.

'Do your jungle walk, then, come back,' he said, 'but I'll be waiting for you. Look at you.'

He lifted her hands so they could both see the cuts and scratches, then pointed to bruises on her arms.

'I am not a violent man but I could kill the people who made you suffer this way. At least let me wash you, and check there's no infection.'

Ellie could feel her body trembling—from his touch and from the thought of intimacies to come. She wanted to pull back but, though Nik only held her loosely by the hand, something stronger wouldn't let her move away.

This was what commitment was about. You gave all your vulnerabilities to the one you loved and trusted them to guard and protect them—not use them against you as a less committed person might.

'I'll come back,' she whispered, and left him to handle his own skimpy ablutions.

Back in the wash house, Nik had rigged up a curtain across the door, actually two towels hung ingeniously so only the most determined snooper would see inside. His skin was damp and he was wearing shorts, but his chest was bare.

And sprinkled with dark hair so tempting it was all Ellie could do not to run her fingers across it.

'You can look but don't touch,' he ordered, and though he smiled as he spoke, the strain in his voice suggested he was feeling as tense as she was.

She stood in front of him, met his eyes and nodded in reply to the question in his. He reached out and undid the buttons on her shirt, then slid it off her shoulders, a soft intake of breath the only indication of his reaction to her bare breasts.

'No bra—you shameless woman!' he teased softly, his eyes on her body now, not her face.

'I used it to wipe the blood off my hands and couldn't get it clean,' she whispered, surprised to find her voice had lost its strength.

She saw his quick frown, but then he was untying the vine that held her trousers up, and as the over-large garment slid to puddle at her feet, a burst of loud Greek curses made her step backwards in surprise. She tripped on the trousers and would have fallen if Nik hadn't caught her and held her upright.

'Damn their black souls to hell.' He cursed in English now, one arm around her while his hands gently touched the scrapes and welts across her pale skin, and the blue bruises from the boot of the soldier who'd kicked her awake.

'They're superficial, Nik,' she assured him, though she was feeling shaky with the emotion that charged the air in the small room. 'I fell a lot the night they brought me here, and things jabbed into me.'

'Because they tied your hands!' he growled, his keen eyes finding the friction marks around her wrists. 'And that animal out there thinks I'll help his wife.'

Ellie sighed. Why did men have to go all macho at exactly the wrong moment?

'He's not an animal. Misguided, yes, but he's worried sick about his wife. All he wanted was to have someone with her when she gave birth—someone who'd know what to do if there was a problem.'

'He should have thought of that before he started this damn war!' Nik said, though he'd recovered sufficiently to begin bathing her, using, she noticed, his shirt, rolled into a soft pad.

'Well, he didn't,' Ellie reminded him, realising she would have to be the calm, unemotional one in this current crisis. 'And that's not the issue. All we have to do is stick to our guns about not attending Ursula until peace talks are under way.'

'So easy,' Nik mocked. 'Especially when they start cutting off your toes.'

He was washing her legs now, having done the toes, and as he worked his way up, Ellie's body became more and more aroused, though she knew sex was the last thing they should be considering. Staying alive was far more important. Staying alive should take precedence over everything.

But it was hard to think of staying alive—no, it was impossible to think of not being alive when Nik's hands were on her skin, and Nik's body was calling to hers with such seductive sweetness.

He finished washing her, examined her wounds and agreed they were superficial, then kissed a bruise on her shoulder. From there it was only a matter of time until kisses explored more of her body, awakening it to such a frenzy of desire she pulled up the trousers, wrapped her shirt around her shoulders, thrust her feet into her sandals and with unseemly haste made her way back to the lock-up—certain Nik was right behind her, praying he'd find a way to make the door secure.

'This was not the way I wanted to first make love to you,' he said, much later, when the wild-fire of desire had been at least temporarily quenched.

Ellie, drowsing in his arms, smiled.

'Let's just hope it's not the last time,' she murmured, and nuzzled his shoulder.

'Why did you cut your hair?'

It was such a strange question, coming in this moment of such wonderful repletion, that she repeated it in her head before answering. Then she shrugged.

'It seemed like time. You said once you thought I kept my hair long for Dave, and that was true. He liked it long and it seemed such a small thing to do for him, though it wasn't a small thing when I went away to places like Afghanistan where there was no water to wash it. Anyway, it stayed long, and I stayed locked in a kind of vacuum that wasn't grief so much as emptiness.'

He hugged her closer, offering silent empathy, but she could feel the tightness in his body and knew he was waiting for the rest of the story.

'Then, when I was part of the first KidCare team you put together, something happened. It was as if the vacuum had cracked open and stuff kept creeping in.'

'Stuff?'

She wriggled with embarrassment, certain he knew what she was talking about but not wanting to confirm it with words.

'Feelings,' she said gruffly. 'Not straight away. Not all the time. But towards the end, feelings I couldn't keep pretending were just friendship.'

'Towards me?'

Nik sounded so astounded she went all defensive.

'Of course towards you,' she snapped. 'Do you think they might have been towards Paul, or Jack, or Frank?'

'They might have been,' Nik said mildly, but Ellie could see a smile curling on his lips and knew he was feeling pleased by the revelation. But as she watched, the smile disappeared and two parallel frown lines appeared between his brows.

She turned to see Rani had appeared in the doorway.

'Come out. We have decided. The woman will go down and talk to Arwon. She will arrange a meeting in the town. He may bring four of his men and we will bring four of ours. The meeting will be at midday tomorrow. The woman will return to camp to say the meeting is on, then you…' he pointed at Nik '…will accompany us to the meeting.'

'I'll go down and arrange the meeting,' Nik suggested. 'Ellie's exhausted.'

'She should not have run away,' Rani said, and the implacability in his tone suggested argument would be a waste of breath.

'I'll go,' Ellie said, and she kissed Nik one more time. 'I'll make sure we stop at the mine site, let the others know we're OK, and get some gear in case we have to deliver Ursula's baby up here in the jungle.'

Though she wouldn't have admitted it, she was glad of an excuse to get away, not from the camp as much as from Nik.

How embarrassing to have told him about how she'd begun to feel on the last mission they'd shared. And though she was reasonably sure he'd talked of love and marriage in the cell in the dark the previous night, she didn't think things said under such circumstances could really be taken at face value.

So making the trek back to camp would take her mind off all the personal chaos.

CHAPTER TWELVE

NIK waited and worried, then, deciding worrying was a waste of mental energy, began to consider his role as arbiter between the warring factions. He had walked a little way down the track with Ellie and her guards then his guard had turned him back. He'd been sitting outside the lock-up doing his worrying, but now he had a purpose he needed a pen and paper to jot down some thoughts.

Ursula provided him with both, though sulkily, demanding first he examine her.

'No point without a foetal heart monitor, which Ellie is bringing back,' he said, determined to stick to Ellie's plan of no consultation without co-operation.

He took his new acquisitions back to the little hut and settled once again outside the door.

Then, as he did when working out a budget for one of his clinics or aid missions, he started to write down any expenses the island nation might incur. Importing food would be the highest cost, and if the locals wanted a modicum of civilised living, then building supplies and household items would come next.

In his own work, all he had in the income column was the money he would donate, but here the people had a priceless asset. If they could get the mine working again, in such a way all the parties were happy with the division of the profits, then the islanders should never know hardship again.

He thought of the Arab states, where oil brought even the poorest people luxuries, and knew Ellie was right to have taken the stand she had. What use to save the life of one infant while adults were killing each other and children were playing war?

But thinking of Ellie's stand brought the anxiety back again, so he started on more figures, working out his own income and expenditure once he'd forfeited the shipping company shares. It would be tight, but he doubted Ellie would care. In fact, if what she'd said was true—about them being from such different worlds—she might be delighted to know just how poor they'd be.

The high-pitched scream brought him out of his reverie, and Rani's arrival at his door told him it was big trouble.

'My wife—she's hurt.'

And for all the bold words he and Ellie had spoken earlier about not helping, Nik led the way across the clearing.

Ursula was doubled up on the floor, writhing in pain, but as they entered she looked up.

'I fell. It hurt. My waters broke. The baby's coming. I can feel his leg.'

Nik knelt beside her and lifted the woman's wet, blood-streaked skirt. What he saw made him blanch with fear for the unborn child.

'Prolapsed cord,' he said quietly to Rani. 'Do you have any sterile gloves?'

Rani shook his head, and Nik cursed himself for not thinking to carry at least basic supplies on his 'rescue Ellie' adventure.

'Disinfectant? Alcohol? Anything you can produce right now?'

Rani reached behind the bed and handed Nik a bottle of whisky.

Better to risk infection than damage to the baby, Nik told himself as he splashed whisky across his fingers, then, explaining to Ursula what he was doing, he carefully slid two fingers into the vagina, feeling for the tight little bottom and pushing it upward so the cord wasn't compromised.

He tried to picture what was going on inside the woman's womb. What he felt was definitely a bottom, not a head, so Ellie had been right about it being breech.

He knew it was possible to deliver a breech baby with a prolapsed cord, but didn't want to try it in a jungle camp with no instruments.

'This is a dangerous situation,' he said to Rani. 'We've got to get her to the hospital. Get your men to make a stretcher of some kind. We'll carry Ursula down the track to where you keep your vehicles and drive her to the hospital from there. There's no time to argue.'

Rani hesitated for a moment then took off, and Nik breathed a sigh of relief.

If he positioned Ursula on her knees in a head-down position on the stretcher, the baby's weight and gravity would ease the tension on the cord, which was just as well as he didn't fancy making the long trek down the mountain with his fingers where they were.

Rani must have sent a runner on ahead, because Ellie and the men who'd been escorting her met them while they were still negotiating the track. Quickly he explained, then he handed Ellie the whisky bottle.

'Only antiseptic available,' he said. 'Wash your fingers and take my place.'

Ursula was in obvious distress, her regular contractions made more painful by the awkward position she was in. Ellie turned to Rani, who was walking beside the stretcher.

'There's an old man in the hospital who smokes some kind of leaves in his pipe. It makes him go to sleep. What are they?'

Rani looked curiously at her for a moment, then flashed a smile and disappeared into the jungle that crowded the almost invisible path. He returned with a handful of green leaves.

'You can chew them, too. They are forbidden to my men but, yes, they might help Ursula.'

'As long as they don't affect her muscles,' Nik warned, and Ellie nodded, then turned towards him.

'Would it matter? Is she going to be able to deliver normally.'

Nik shook his head.

'Not a hope, I'd say.' He grinned at Ellie. 'Go ahead, Rani. Give her the leaves.'

They reached the old Jeep and arranged themselves and Ursula into the back of it. With Ursula in a knee-chest position, the pressure on the cord should be negligible, but as her contractions got stronger and her muscles pushed the baby towards her cervix, it was still necessary to maintain touch to keep the cord from being compromised and blood supply to the baby being cut off.

Nik and Ellie took turns to check the position and integrity of the cord, and by the time they reached the mine site Ellie felt exhausted. But she was also worried about Rani and Ursula—having brought them into possible danger.

With Arwon and his men back around the mine site, would full-scale war break out right there?

And Nik still had to do the Caesar and save the baby—it was she and Nik who'd be in danger if anything went wrong.

Nothing did, and less than an hour after reaching the camp, Ursula was in the camp bed in the living room, her proud husband sitting beside her, cradling in his arms a healthy baby girl.

Nik put his arm around Ellie and led her out of the room, giving the little family some privacy. He drew her close to his body, thinking this might be a good time to kiss her—to celebrate the joy of a new life with a taste of honey from her lips. If he announced to the others that they were engaged, would she feel comfortable about shifting into his room?

Of course, he'd have to find somewhere else for Jack to sleep. Jasmine probably wouldn't want the older man in her room—

'Now we *have* to sort out this stupid war situation.'

For a moment Ellie's words didn't make sense, then he realised just how far apart their thoughts had shifted.

'Right now?' he asked, knowing Jack would be at lunch and their room empty.

But he knew what she would say.

'Of course we do. Here's a newborn baby— do you want her growing up into a world of war? Living up there in the jungle and going in fear of her life if she ventures out of it?'

Nik turned, pulled her into his arms and kissed her anyway—just a brief kiss. Surely he deserved that much!

'No, of course I don't,' he murmured, thinking if his lips stayed close to her skin, they'd surely kiss again. 'I've some ideas. I'll talk to Arwon and get him and Rani together. I'll even contact the pilot and get him to bring over a representative of the mining company. I did some figures—worked it out—but first, the future Mrs Conias, may we, please, talk about us?'

'Us?' She pulled away from him, and what he saw in her eyes made his heart stop beating.

'Oh, Nik, I know we talked about how we feel, but there can't be any us. You must know that. Look at the work you do—at the good you achieve in so many ways and so many places. Even with fundraising we'd never achieve the amounts you're contributing now from the shipping company. How would I feel, knowing I'd selfishly married you and in doing so denied so many children a chance of health and happiness? A life? A future?'

Nik stared at her, unable to believe what he was hearing.

'But I can talk to Lena—we can work it out,' he growled, the hot anger he tried so hard to control rising at the intransigence of the woman he loved.

She leaned against him and stopped his protests with another kiss, then whispered her argument against his lips.

'You know we'd both be unhappy—feel we'd cheated somehow—buying our own happiness at such great cost to others. It would cast a shadow between us that would grow darker every time we read or heard of places where we could be helping. Isn't KidCare too important to both of us to put our personal happiness ahead of it?'

He should have throttled her the other day, he decided. It would have saved him all this anguish! He eased away from her, trying desperately to keep a lid on his emotions until he found a calm, rational argument with which to refute her assertions.

'I need to use the radio,' he said, the icy control he was exerting frosting the words.

Then he walked away.

Jack was in the storeroom where they kept the radio, sitting at a table with a sheaf of notes in front of him.

'You might let me know next time you go rushing off into the jungle to rescue your woman,' he grumbled at Nik. 'There's a dozen messages come in for you. Radio wasn't working for a while. Carl fixed a new aerial on it and suddenly the whole world wants to talk to you.'

'The whole world wants to talk to me?' Ellie's rejection must have boiled his brain. Nothing was making sense. Though he did refute part of the message. 'And she's not my woman!'

Jack ignored that comment.

'Seems the price of platinum's gone through the roof, and a number of mining companies are interested in restarting operations right here in

Erireka,' he said. 'And word leaked out to the press that you were actually on the island, so reporters thought you might be able to give them some local colour.'

'As if!' Nik muttered, waving away the information as easily as he might have dismissed a gnat annoying him. 'But I do want to talk to someone from the mining company. The island needs the mine, and the warring factions here need someone to talk sense into them—as well as someone from the outside world on their side.'

'And you'd be that someone?' Jack asked, and Nik glared at him.

'I know we don't usually get politically involved, but this is for the children. Would KidCare really be doing its job if it didn't at least try to sort things out?'

Jack shrugged, then flipped through the messages, lifting up one slip of paper and handing it to Nik.

'KidCare won't be doing anything if you don't get on to Lena. She's been trying to contact you for days.'

Nik felt his stomach contract into a small, hard knot. He couldn't speak to Lena until he'd sorted out his feelings. Marrying her for the sake of KidCare had seemed a reasonable option back when his father had died. After all, arranged marriages weren't rare in his culture. And as long as the partners had respect for each other, then friendship, and possibly even love, would grow between them, and the marriage would be a success.

He took a turn around the small room, his thoughts too tortured for him to stand still.

But what promise of success was there if he married one woman knowing he loved another?

'Perhaps you should find out what Lena wants of you,' Jack suggested. 'Have you considered she might not find you the catch the nurse does?'

'The nurse has just refused my offer of marriage,' Nik said curtly, but maybe Jack's suggestion had merit. Maybe Lena wanted out as much as he did!

'I need to think,' he said to Jack. 'I'll be back in half an hour—try to track down Lena so I can speak to her then. And leaf through the notes from reporters. Choose one from a responsible news agency and have him ready to speak to me as well.'

He left the storeroom, going first to check on Ursula, hoping Ellie might be there.

'She went to bed,' Jasmine told him. 'Poor thing, she was so exhausted she was crying.'

Ellie crying? And probably not from exhaustion. He hardened his heart against the pity he felt and went in search of her, finding her sitting on the bed, her elbows propped on her knees, her head in her hands.

'Come on,' he said. 'I need your help.'

And though every atom in his body wanted to take her in his arms and comfort her, he spoke briskly and impersonally, knowing she'd respond automatically—a nurse taking orders from a doctor.

'More trouble?' she asked, pushing to her feet, her voice husky with the tears that still stained her cheeks.

'You could say that,' he said, taking her hand and leading her out of the house.

The car was just outside the door, keys, as ever, dangling from the ignition. He held the door open for her, then walked around the bonnet and got in, knowing she must be both physically and emotionally exhausted or she'd be questioning his actions.

He drove swiftly down to the town, through streets already deserted, as if the setting sun was a signal to go inside. Stopping by the long pier where the Blue Funnel Line had once loaded ore, he leaned across her and opened the door.

'Out!' he said, and though she glanced his way and recovered sufficient energy to raise her eyebrows at the order, she didn't argue.

He took her hand and walked her to the end of the pier where they could look down into the deep, dark blue water.

'Sit!' he said, pointing to a bollard.

She smiled at him, and although it was a tired smile, it made his heart beat faster and sent fire flickering along his nerves.

'Come! Out! Sit! Are you going to say "Stay"? Am I so well trained you know I'll obey your commands?'

'Well trained?' he huffed, still coping with the smile. 'You're the most ill-disciplined nurse I've ever had the misfortune to work with. But I needed to think, and you help me do that. And I need to know some things.'

His heart quaked, uncertain now that this approach would work—terrified she might not want him anyway...

Ellie saw pain and confusion in his eyes, and knew she'd put the pain there. Where the confusion had come from she wasn't sure, but it hurt her to see Nik, who was usually so much in control, confused.

'What things?' she asked softly.

He took a deep breath and looked out to where the sinking sun had turned the sea a vivid scarlet.

'Do you love me?'

Time for truth. She didn't hesitate.

'Yes!'

He turned back to her and smiled as if greatly relieved.

'Enough to marry me if there were no extenuating circumstances?'

'Yes,' she said again, listening to her own heart, revealing its truth in one simple word.

'Good,' he said, then he pulled her to her feet and kissed her.

Her lips parted hungrily, and for an instant he felt the sensual reaction raging through his body, then she stopped, easing away, one hand resting on his chest as if to prevent him kissing her again.

'Has your fiancée died and left you the shipping company?' she asked, running the fingers of her other hand through his hair, as if she needed to touch him as much as he needed to touch her.

'No, but the price of platinum has gone through the roof. Companies are competing for the mine—companies who'll make a lot of money—companies who might be looking for tax breaks—for worthy causes to whom they can donate some of their profits.'

Ellie felt hope rise like champagne bubbles inside her.

'You think…?'

'We can try,' Nik told her. 'We'll need both Arwon and Rani on side, but both are good men at heart and I can't help feeling they'd like to put Erireka on the map, not just for its platinum but for its humanitarian efforts as well. The company donates the money but in the name of the Erirekan people. We can have an entire nation supporting KidCare!'

He was so excited Ellie couldn't put a damper on things by suggesting this might not work out, but when she thought about it, walking back down the pier, Nik's arm warm against her back, her head resting on his shoulder, she realised that if ever anyone could pull it off, Nik could.

He had the foresight to foresee any potential arguments, and the intelligence to find ways to solve them, and he had such obvious dedication to the organisation he'd founded, it shone like the last bright wink of the setting sun.

Shone like the hope that now arose in her heart…

CHAPTER THIRTEEN

THEY were seated at a table, set incongruously beneath waving coconut palms—eight islanders, the second in command of the mining company, a specialist in international law, a reporter from a worldwide news agency, Nik, and, at the end of the table, three determined women.

Rani and Arwon had agreed—once Nik had pointed out how bad anything but agreement would look to the rest of the world—that the fighting would stop and the islanders would co-operate with the mining company, provided their demands for a fair share of the mine income were accepted. Now all that remained was for the division of the money to be agreed and a date for the reopening of the mine to be set.

'The funding of KidCare must also be written into the agreement,' Ellie reminded them all.

'And the agreement should show the donations are from the people of Erireka,' Ursula added.

'*And* the Blue Funnel Line. If we're shipping the ore, we'll match the contribution.'

Nik smiled at the woman he'd got to know over the last difficult weeks of negotiation, the woman who had told him, when he'd finally got through to her on the radio, that she'd met a man—the international lawyer, as it turned out—and would fight the condition in his father's will.

Ursula was arguing with Lena now, pointing out they'd want a good deal with the shipping costs and Blue Funnel needn't think they'd get preferential treatment.

But it was the woman between the arguing pair who drew most of Nik's attention—the woman he would marry tomorrow, here beneath the palm trees, by the azure water of the harbour—the woman who had forced him to step beyond the boundaries he'd set himself in order to win her for a bride.

'It seems like weeks since we've been alone together,' he said much later, when they were back at camp, sitting on the back steps of the hospital because she'd insisted on doing night duty, and he'd come to report the agreements were all signed.

Tomorrow she'd be his, and though emotionally he knew there was so much more to their relationship than the physical joy they shared, something deep inside him was excited by the knowledge of elemental possession—that she'd be 'his woman', to touch, to taste, to know in every sense.

'You've been too busy with your other three women,' Ellie reminded him—obviously not in tune with his thoughts tonight because she snuggled closer to his body, tempting the elemental man within.

Fortunately her words distracted him.

'Other *three* women? Lena, yes, I've had to get to know her, and Ursula, once she decided the war should end, but who's the third?'

Ellie kissed him lightly on the lips.

'Don't think I haven't seen you sneaking in to the house to cuddle baby Rose.'

Nik drew her closer, kissing her ear.

'You have to admit she's about the cutest baby you've ever seen.'

Ellie smiled, and turned to kiss his cheek.

'Fortunately, her parents agree with you. I'm sure without her as a catalyst to get things settled, the peace talks and mine negotiations could have gone on for months.'

'It seems like months to me,' Nik told her, then kissed her lips. 'Months and months,' he murmured against them, running his hands lightly over her arms so shivers of desire sprang to life in every cell of her body. 'And don't go thinking we're going to get politically involved in any other country. This was a one-off, remember.'

Ellie captured his roving hands. She'd just checked on her patients—fewer now the chickenpox outbreak was nearly over—and could afford a few minutes of companionship with Nik. But only a few minutes!

'Don't blame me for the political stuff—you were just as determined to stop the stupid fighting as I was. I saw you organising that soccer game with the kids when you should have been catching up on your sleep, back when the young girl was first injured, and I heard you telling Jack he had to supervise the children's play and make sure the war games stopped.'

She kissed his cheek again, so proud of what he'd achieved, so full of love for him she wondered her body could contain all the emotion. 'You told me love would win out in the end—remember? That night we looked up at the stars?'

Ellie tipped her head back to see them once again—bright lights in the firmament—as bright as the love she felt for Nik—shining as KidCare would shine on in places where its services were needed.

'And it did,' Nik said, 'but not without a lot of input from a very special woman. *My* very special woman!'

'I love you, Nik,' she said quietly.

'And I love you,' he answered, making a pledge of the simple words before turning so he could he seal them with a kiss.

A honeyed kiss…

MEDICAL ROMANCE™

Large Print

Titles for the next six months…

October

THE DOCTOR'S RESCUE MISSION	Marion Lennox
THE LATIN SURGEON	Laura MacDonald
DR CUSACK'S SECRET SON	Lucy Clark
HER SURGEON BOSS	Abigail Gordon

November

HER EMERGENCY KNIGHT	Alison Roberts
THE DOCTOR'S FIRE RESCUE	Lilian Darcy
A VERY SPECIAL BABY	Margaret Barker
THE CHILDREN'S HEART SURGEON	Meredith Webber

December

THE DOCTOR'S SPECIAL TOUCH	Marion Lennox
CRISIS AT KATOOMBA HOSPITAL	Lucy Clark
THEIR VERY SPECIAL MARRIAGE	Kate Hardy
THE HEART SURGEON'S PROPOSAL	Meredith Webber

MILLS & BOON®

Live the emotion

0905 LP 2P P1 Medical

MEDICAL ROMANCE™

Large Print

January

THE CELEBRITY DOCTOR'S PROPOSAL Sarah Morgan
UNDERCOVER AT CITY HOSPITAL Carol Marinelli
A MOTHER FOR HIS FAMILY   Alison Roberts
A SPECIAL KIND OF CARING   Jennifer Taylor

February

HOLDING OUT FOR A HERO   Caroline Anderson
HIS UNEXPECTED CHILD   Josie Metcalfe
A FAMILY WORTH WAITING FOR   Margaret Barker
WHERE THE HEART IS   Kate Hardy

March

THE ITALIAN SURGEON   Meredith Webber
A NURSE'S SEARCH AND RESCUE Alison Roberts
THE DOCTOR'S SECRET SON   Laura MacDonald
THE FOREVER ASSIGNMENT   Jennifer Taylor

MILLS & BOON®

Live the emotion

0905 LP 2P P2 Medical